"MISSION TO MONTE CARLO"

Craig Vandervelt, handsome son of the richest man in America is begged by his cousin, the Marquess of Lansdowne, the British Foreign Secretary, to undertake a secret mission.

He is on his way to Monte Carlo and the Marquess tells him that one of Britain's most important agents in India, Randall Sare, has unexpectedly arrived there, then disappeared.

He also tells Craig that a beautiful Russian Countess suspected of being a spy is continually in the company of Lord Neasdon, a newcomer to the Foreign Office, who may inadvertently give her information regarding the British interests in Tibet.

How Craig sets out to solve these two problems, how he encounters danger and treachery, yet finds the idealistic love he has always sought is told in this 321st book by Barbara Cartland.

Other Books by Barbara Cartland
Romantic Novels, over 300, the most recently
published being:

Autobiographical and Biographical

Historical:

Sociology:

YOU IN THE HOME
THE FASCINATING FORTIES
MARRIAGE FOR MODERNS
BE VIVID, BE VITAL
LOVE, LIFE AND SEX
VITAMINS FOR VITALITY
HUSBANDS AND WIVES
ETIQUETTE
THE MANY FACETS OF LOVE
SEX AND THE TEENAGER
THE BOOK OF CHARM
LIVING TOGETHER
THE YOUTH SECRET
THE MAGIC OF HONEY

BARBARA CARTLAND'S BOOK OF BEAUTY AND HEALTH
MEN ARE WONDERFUL

Cookery:

BARBARA CARTLAND'S HEALTH FOOD COOKERY BOOK
FOOD FOR LOVE
MAGIC OF HONEY COOKBOOK
RECIPES FOR LOVERS

Editor of:

THE COMMON PROBLEMS BY RONALD CARTLAND (with a
preface by the Rt. Hon. The Earl of Selborne, P.C.)
BARBARA CARTLAND'S LIBRARY OF LOVE.
BARBARA CARTLAND'S LIBRARY OF ANCIENT WISDOM
"WRITTEN WITH LOVE", passionate love letters selected by
Barbara Cartland

Drama:

BLOOD MONEY
FRENCH DRESSING

Philosophy:

TOUCH THE STARS

Radio Operetta:

THE ROSE AND THE VIOLET (music by Mark Lubbock).
Performed in 1942.

Radio Plays:

THE CAGED BIRD: An episode in the Life of Elizabeth
Empress of Austria. Performed in 1957.

General:

BARBARA CARTLAND'S BOOK OF USELESS
INFORMATION, with a Foreword by The Earl
Mountbatten of Burma.
(In Aid of the United World Colleges.)

LOVE AND LOVERS (Picture Book)
THE LIGHT OF LOVE (Prayer Book)

BARBARA CARTLAND'S SCRAPBOOK,
in Aid of the Royal Photographic Museum.

Verse:

LINES ON LIFE AND LOVE.

Music:

An Album of Love Songs sung with the Royal
Philharmonic Orchestra.

Magazines:

BARBARA CARTLAND'S WORLD OF ROMANCE (published
in the U.S.A.)

Special Publication:

LOVE AT THE HELM.
Inspired and helped by Admiral of the Fleet Earl
Mountbatten of Burma, in Aid of the Mountbatten
Memorial Trust.

Mission to Monte Carlo

Barbara Cartland

CORGI BOOKS

MISSION TO MONTE CARLO

A CORGI BOOK 0 552 12247 5

First publication in Great Britain

PRINTING HISTORY
Corgi edition published 1983

This book is set in 10/11 Plantin

Corgi Books are published by
Transworld Publishers Ltd.,
Century House, 61–63 Uxbridge Road,
Ealing, London W5 5SA
Made and printed by Elsnerdruck GmbH, Berlin

About The Author

Barbara Cartland, the world's most famous romantic novelist, who is also an historian, playwright, lecturer, political speaker and television personality, has now written over 300 books and sold over 200 million over the world.

She has also had many historical works published and has written four autobiographies as well as the biographies of her mother and that of her brother, Ronald Cartland, who was the first Member of Parliament to be killed in the last war. This book has a preface by Sir Winston Churchill and has just been republished with an introduction by Sir Arthur Bryant.

She has recently completed a novel, 'Love at the Helm' with the help and inspiration of the late Admiral of the Fleet, the Earl Mountbatten of Burma. This is being sold for the Mountbatten Memorial Trust.

Miss Cartland in 1978 sang an an Album of Love Songs with the Royal Philharmonic Orchestra.

In 1976 by writing twenty-one books, she broke the world record and has continued for the following five years with 24, 20, 23, 24, and 23. In the Guinness Book of Records she is listed as the world's top-selling author.

In private life Barbara Cartland, who is a Dame of the Order of St. John of Jerusalem, Chairman of the St. John Council in Hertfordshire and Deputy President of the St. John Ambulance Brigade, has fought for better conditions and salaries for Midwives and Nurses.

She has championed the cause for old people, had the law altered regarding gypsies and founded the first

Romany Gypsy camp in the world.

Barbara Cartland is deeply interested in Vitamin Therapy and is President of the National Association for Health.

Her designs "Decorating with Love" are being sold all over the U.S.A. and the National Home Fashions League made her, in 1981, "Woman of Achievement."

Helena Rubinstein have just introduced three Barbara Cartland fragrances in America, called after three of her novels, "Love Wins", "The Heart Triumphant", and "Moments of Love". Also fifty-four newspapers in the United States and several countries in Europe carry the strip cartoons of her novels.

Author's Note

Monte Carlo in the last years of the last century was the smartest place in Europe. The guest list to the small Principality reads like a mixture of the Almanak de Goetha and Debrett.

Yet the division between the Social classes was unbridgable. During her honeymoon in Monte Carlo after her marriage to the 9th Duke of Marlborough, the Duchess, formerly Consuelo Vanderbilt, pointed out to him the elegance and beauty of some of the women to be seen in the Casino.

To her surprise he forbade her to mention them and not to recognise the men who accompanied them, even if she had dined with them in the same party the previous night.

Only gradually did she understand the lovely women were the leading Courtesans of Europe.

Other guests were the fascinating and extravagant Grand Duke Serge of Russia, the Grand Duke Nicolas, the Aga Khan, the beautiful, alluring Lily Langtry, the Duke of Montrose, the Prince of Denmark and inevitably the Prince of Wales.

Countless novels, plays and thrillers have been written about Monte Carlo but there is no other place in the whole world which is synonymous with Kings and Princes, Grand Dukes, tricksters, cocottes, cocaine, systems and suicides.

CHAPTER ONE

1900

The carriage drew up outside the Foreign Office and a tall man got out and walked in through the massive pillared door.

As soon as he appeared and before his servant could speak a young man in a frock-coat came hurrying forward.

'Mr. Vandervelt?'

The newcomer nodded.

'The Secretary of State for Foreign Affairs is waiting for you, Sir.'

'Thank you,' Craig Vandervelt replied.

He was escorted along the high-ceilinged, rather gloomy corridors until his escort opened a door into a large, impressive office.

Seated at a desk in front of a window which overlooked a small garden at the rear of the building was the Marquess of Lansdowne.

A very good-looking man, already going grey, he rose to his feet as Craig Vandervelt was announced and held out his hand.

'I only heard yesterday, Craig,' he said, 'that you were in London. I am delighted to see you.'

'How are you, My Lord? I am on my way to Monte Carlo,' Craig Vandervelt replied.

There was something almost defensive in his tone, as though he was warning the Marquess that he was only passing through England.

As if he understood the Secretary of State said:

'Sit down. I have a lot to tell you.'

Craig Vandervelt laughed.

'That is what I was afraid of!'

He seated himself however in a comfortable chair, crossed his legs and seemed very much at his ease.

The Marquess sat down opposite him thinking that, as a great many women had thought before him, it would be hard to find a better-looking, more attractive young man anywhere in the world.

It was not surprising. Craig Vandervelt's father came from Texas, and it was his astute and brilliant brain which had turned what had been the Vandervelt misfortune into one of the greatest fortunes in America.

His mother, a daughter of the Duke of Newcastle, had been one of the great beauties of her generation. It was therefore not surprising that their only son would be not only extremely good-looking and irresistibly attractive, but also, although not many people were aware of it, had a brain which matched his father's.

Because he had no inclination to add to the enormous wealth his family had already accumulated, Craig had, from the world's point of view, become a 'playboy'.

He travelled extensively, enjoyed himself not only in the great Capitals which catered for rich young men, but also in more obscure, unknown parts of the earth, where a man had to prove his manhood rather than rely entirely on his pocket-book.

'I was thinking about you only a few days ago,' the Marquess said, 'and then, almost as if my prayers were answered, I was told you were actually here and I was wondering how I could get in touch with you.'

'I am staying with my cousin in Park Lane.'

'I realise that now,' the Marquess said, 'but I had some anxious hours trying other places before I ran you to ground.'

'You are making me feel rather like a fox,' Craig protested, 'and I have already told you, My Lord, I am on my way to Monte Carlo.'

'That is what I might have expected,' the Marquess said with a smile, 'I am told that the Season there is gayer than it has ever been, and the beauties of the *Monde* and the *demi-Monde* glittering with jewels and covered in ospreys are dazzling!'

Craig threw back his head and laughed.

'I sense a note of envy in your voice, My Lord. You should accompany me to Monte Carlo.'

'There is nothing I would enjoy more,' the Marquess replied. 'Unfortunately, I have to be here at the moment, although doubtless you will find the Prince of Wales amongst other Royal visitors at the green tables.'

Craig smiled as if it was only to be expected, and the Marquess said:

'As it happens, if you had not been going to Monte Carlo, that is where I was going to ask you to go, and to cancel any other plans you had made.'

There was a little silence. Then Craig said with a different look in his dark eyes:

'You speak as if there is something urgent.'

'It is very urgent,' the Marquess replied quietly, 'and I believe that only you can help me.'

Craig did not answer.

He knew the Marquess would not speak in such a way unless what he required of him was something of international importance.

In fact the Marquess of Lansdowne, before he became Secretary of State for Foreign Affairs, had enlisted Craig Vandervelt's help in ways which would have confounded, if they had known about it, those who looked on the American millionaire as an incessant seeker of pleasure.

It was the Marquess who had sensed that Craig was becoming bored with the role that had been thrust upon him and was growing cynical about his success with the women who flocked around him like bees round a honey-pot.

The Marquess therefore enlisted his help in a small but important mission which concerned the German ambition for supremacy in Europe.

Craig had played his part so brilliantly that he had been thanked for what he did not only by the Prime Minister, but also by the Queen.

13

The Marquess had continued to enlist the young American's assistance in one way or another again and again.

Because it was so secret and so very different in every way from his other pursuits, Craig had found himself intrigued and amused by what became at times a very dangerous pastime.

Twice he had missed by a hair's breadth being shot, and once an assailant's knife had been diverted by a split second of good timing.

The thrill of it, and the excitement of what he thought of as 'dicing with death', was something which had become a part of his life, and he knew now that whatever the Marquess asked of him, he would agree to do it.

The Marquess however seemed to have a little difficulty in choosing the words in which to explain the task that lay ahead.

As if he knew Craig was waiting almost impatiently he said:

'Forgive me if I seem hesitant. It is not because I am keeping secrets from you, but finding it difficult to explain how very little I know of the brief I should have prepared before you arrived.'

'The first thing to do,' Craig said with an amused smile, 'is to tell me what is the name of the enemy this time.'

He thought as he spoke that this was extremely important because on one occasion when he was helping the Marquess he had been misinformed, or rather not told specifically, who was against him.

Only his intuition and his sixth sense had saved him from walking into a skilfully prepared trap from which it would have been impossible to extricate himself.

'The difficulty is,' the Marquess said in reply to his question, 'that as yet I have only suspicions rather than facts to justify my conviction that you are desperately needed in Monte Carlo at this particular moment.'

'Then let me hear your suspicions,' Craig suggested. 'I am quite certain, My Lord, that I shall find them fully justified when the time comes, by something more lethal than a bow and arrow.'

The Marquess laughed, but there was not much

amusement in the sound.

'The trouble is, Craig,' he said, 'I am very apprehensive about what I am letting you in for. Our own agents so far have come up with very little and, quite frankly, the men we have in Monte Carlo at the moment are unable to move in the right circles, where I believe they are needed.'

'That, at any rate, should present no difficulty!' Craig remarked dryly.

No-one knew better than he did that because he was so rich he was welcome wherever he went.

Yet at twenty-nine years of age it was a pity that when crowned Kings linked their arms with his, and Queens held out their soft hands in welcome, he inevitably wondered whether their enthusiasm for him was a response to his charm or to his unlimited bank balance.

As if the Marquess knew what he was thinking he said:

'You are popular everywhere you go, Craig, and that is your great advantage from my professional point of view.'

He lowered his voice instinctively as he said:

'I believe and hope that nobody has the slightest idea outside these walls that your connection with me is anything other than that through your mother, we are related. And they assume that it is only your search for amusement which takes you to strange places.'

'I hope you are right, My Lord,' Craig replied. 'If it were not so, in some of the situations in which I have been involved I would not have been likely to last long.'

The Marquess frowned.

'Perhaps I am wrong, Craig, in asking so much of you,' he said, 'but I need hardly tell you how useful you have been, and how grateful we are.'

His voice deepened as he continued:

'No-one else, and I mean no-one else, could have obtained the information which you have given us and saved us from being involved in disastrous circumstances which might have had far-reaching consequences for the peace of the world.'

'Thank you,' Craig said quietly, 'and now suppose you tell me exactly what you want this time.'

15

'I wish I knew,' the Marquess replied, 'but let me give you an outline.'

Craig listened attentively as he began:

'As you understand because you have helped us before, our position in India appears to be threatened by Russian advances in Central Asia.'

Craig nodded and the Marquess continued:

'Because Russia extends her Sovereignty towards Afghanistan, we have pushed the Frontiers of India further to the West and the North-West.'

This was so well known to Craig that he did not even trouble to murmur agreement, and the Marquess continued:

'Tibet, once dominated by China, is still independent and very hostile to outsiders, but we are worried.'

Now Craig bent forward.

'Why?'

The Marquess dropped his voice even lower almost as if he suspected the walls had ears.

'A coded message from the Viceroy,' he said, 'has told us that he believes a secret Treaty exists between Russia and China giving the former special rights in Tibet.'

'It seems almost impossible.'

'I agree with you,' the Marquess answered, 'but Lord Curzon is sure that Russia has sent arms to Tibet, and he suspects that there will soon be trouble induced by Russia on India's Tibetan border.'

The Marquess was silent and after a moment Craig said:

'I thought you wanted me to go to Monte Carlo?'

'I do,' the Marquess agreed, 'because I have learned that Randall Sare arrived there three weeks ago without our being aware of it.'

Craig looked up in surprise.

'Randall Sare? I do not believe it! I never thought he would come home. When I last saw him in India he said he intended to live the rest of his life in Tibet.'

'So you told me at the time,' the Marquess said, 'but obviously he has changed his mind, and since he arrived in Monte Carlo without getting in touch with us in any way, I can only think the explanation is that he is in hiding because of the information he carries in his mind.'

'But why Monte Carlo?' Craig asked. 'Why did he not come straight back to England?'

'That is something I do not know,' the Marquess answered. 'I agree with you it seems a strange place to stop, and I never thought that Sare was a likely person to be addicted to gambling.'

'No, that would be impossible,' Craig agreed.

He sat back again in his chair and there was a frown between his eyes as he concentrated.

'I can only think,' he said after a moment, 'that he had some particular reason for disembarking at Villefranche, where whatever ship he was travelling in would have stopped. But if he got as far as that, did he then go on to Monte Carlo?'

'It is too difficult for me to answer,' the Marquess said, 'and that is why I am asking you – no, I am begging you, Craig – to go to Monte Carlo as quickly as you can and find Randall Sare.'

'You mean your people have not been in touch with him?'

'No, they saw him, I think in a street, then lost sight of him before they could make contact.'

'It seems incredible,' Craig murmured, 'and very inefficient.'

'You must not blame our men too harshly,' the Marquess said. 'As the one I interviewed explained, he was told never to intrude on anybody of Randall Sare's importance without being quite sure he would not be detected doing so, or that Sare would welcome the contact.'

'That I can understand,' Craig said. 'But if, as you suspect, he is bringing back information of such importance, he may have gone into hiding until he can shake off his pursuers.'

'That thought did cross my mind,' the Marquess replied. 'It might also account for the fact that he left the ship he was on.'

He paused before he added:

'The sea is a very convenient way of getting rid of anybody who is unwanted.'

17

'I agree,' Craig said, 'but I cannot believe that if Randall Sare was spotted three weeks ago he is still sitting in Monte Carlo.'

'I said he *arrived* three weeks ago,' the Marquess corrected, 'and he was seen a week later. It was after that that one of our men came back to tell me he was there, leaving two others to continue the chase, so to speak. They may of course have found him by this time, but if they have not, then I am praying that you will succeed where they have failed.'

Craig's voice was rather cynical as he said:

'I fear you are being optimistic. Knowing Sare, the sort of places in which he might be hiding are not those I am expected to frequent when I am in Monte Carlo.'

'I am aware of that,' the Marquess said, 'and that brings me to the second part of my mission.'

'What is that?'

'My informant who returned to tell me about Sare also told me that he is somewhat anxious about Lord Neasdon.'

'Do I know him?' Craig asked.

'I do not think you have ever met him because since he is a comparative newcomer to the Foreign Office I thought it would be a great mistake for him to know that you and I have any connection with each other except that we are somewhat distantly related.'

'Of course,' Craig murmured.

'He is quite an attractive man, about ten years older than yourself, and he has worked hard in the Diplomatic Service to get the position in which he is now. Because my predecessor had known him for years and was very fond of him, he was put in line for being accepted here on the permanent staff while he was still serving his time in the Embassies of Europe.'

'I understand.'

'Neasdon is unmarried, although I do not need to tell you that he has had a great number of *affaires de coeur* with the Beauties that are to be found at Marlborough House.'

The Marquess paused for a moment and as Craig did not interrupt he went on:

'Now I understand, there is a new woman in his life, and

18

from all I have heard she may be dangerous.'

'Who is she?' Craig enquired.

'Her name,' the Marquess replied, 'is the Countess Aloya Zladamir.'

'Russian, I presume?'

'I think so, although apparently nobody is quite certain. The Russians here to whom I have mentioned her name casually, have never heard of her.'

'There are, I believe,' Craig said, 'over two million Counts in Russia, so it would be impossible for anybody to be acquainted with all of them!'

The Marquess frowned.

'It only makes your task more difficult.'

'Then I am going to search not only for Sare but also for Aloya Zladamir?'

'Exactly!' the Marquess agreed. 'I am well aware there may be nothing in Neasdon's interest in her. At the same time the Russians are very clever with their spies and are determined to ferret out a great deal we have no wish for them to know. That especially is true of Tibet.'

'Do you think there is any link between Sare and the Countess?'

'None that I know of, but that is for you to find out,' the Marquess replied, 'and I think it would be a mistake for me to give you an introduction to Neasdon. It might be too obvious.'

'I am sure there will be no difficulty in my getting to know him,' Craig said.

'He has a great many friends in Monte Carlo who I am sure will be yours too. All I can beg you, Craig, is if you think that Neasdon looks like being indiscreet in any way to step in and prevent it.'

Craig raised his eyebrows and now there was a definite twinkle in his eyes and a twist to his lips as he asked:

'Are you really suggesting. . . . .?'

'I am merely pointing out,' the Marquess said, 'that if any woman had a choice, I am certain she would prefer a young American millionaire to a rather dull, none too wealthy English Peer!'

Craig laughed.

'This time, My Lord, you really have thought out a melodramatic situation which is more suitable to Drury Lane than the Casino in Monte Carlo!'

'I would not be too sure of that,' the Marquess said, 'and, quite frankly, Craig, I am perturbed.'

'Why?'

'It was only in the last two days that I discovered that in mistaken zeal one of my subordinates informed Neasdon of our concern over Tibet, and that we have under-cover agents who attempt to keep us informed of the Russian attitude in that far-away, little-known country.'

He paused before he went on:

'It seems almost too far-fetched to be anything but sheer melodrama, but if Randall Sare is being shadowed by Russians, and if Neasdon inadvertently reveals to the delectable Countess what information we already have, the two combined would be explosive to the point where the work of years could be undone and a great many lives put in jeopardy.'

'I understand,' Craig said, his eyes twinkling, 'and of course it would be a pleasure to make the acquaintance of the Countess.'

'They tell me she is very beautiful,' the Marquess said with a slight smile.

'Then that at least should make my task more pleasant. Is that all you have to tell me?'

The Marquess rose from his desk.

'I have here the names of our men in Monte Carlo, but as you know, it would be very unwise to contact them unless it is absolutely necessary. They should not know that you have any connection with us. In fact, I hope there is no one in Monte Carlo who will be aware of it.'

'That is how I prefer it,' Craig said. 'If there is one thing I dislike, it is working with other people.'

'I know that, and perhaps that is why you are so successful. At the same time, be careful!'

Craig raised his eye-brows as he took the piece of paper

from the Marquess's hand.

'I do not remember you ever saying that to me before.'

'I am saying it this time. I take the Russian menace very, very seriously. I also believe they will stop at nothing to gain their objectives.'

'You mean India!'

'Yes. They have already shown us how ruthless they can be in Afghanistan, and there is no doubt at all that the money, the weapons and the inciting of the tribesmen on the North-West Frontier all originate from St. Petersburg.'

'You have certainly given me an unusual and intriguing assignment this time,' Craig said. 'I only hope I will not fail you.'

'You have never done so yet,' the Marquess replied, 'and because of your unique position in the social world, there is nobody else who could help me as you can at this particular moment. If you have anything to communicate to me, do it in the usual way. I am certain the code we have used before has not yet been broken.'

'I hope not!'

Craig put the piece of paper in his pocket and held out his hand.

'Thank you,' he said, 'and I mean it! This is just what I needed at a moment when life in New York had become monotonous and for the same reason, I do not wish to stay in London.'

'What you really mean,' the Marquess said, 'is that your heart is unoccupied and that is exactly what I hoped it would be!'

Craig laughed.

'I am not even certain if I have a heart, but shall I say my eyes find the landscape too familiar, and 'pastures new' would be a welcome change.'

The Marquess knew without his saying any more that Craig was really insinuating that he had finished with one love-affair and the lady's place in his life had not been filled.

He had heard too, many woman complaining that Craig Vandervelt was cruel, ruthless and heartless, not to know that

21

he was always the one who was bored first, while the woman who had once engaged his attention was left weeping and bewailing her dismissal.

Because Craig's affairs were always with sophisticated beauties who were safely married, there was no question of his being forced to the altar by an irate father, although occasionally a jealous husband would threaten to 'call him out'.

But in some skilful manner of his own he had managed over the years to avoid any open scandal, though it was impossible to prevent his attractions being whispered about from *Boudoir* to *Boudoir*.

The Marquess having shaken his visitor by the hand, walked to the door and thought as he did so that he not only wished he was young again, but also regretted that when he was the same age as Craig he had let far too many opportunities pass him by.

Then he told himself that as a respectable married man those were not the sort of thoughts he should be having!

Yet all over the world he was quite sure there were men like himself who were envious and jealous of Craig not only as a millionaire, but also as a man.

The door of the office opened, and as if Craig understood the importance of the object of the interview being kept a secret, he said in a voice that could be heard down the corridor:

'Well, goodbye, My Lord. Give my love to all our relatives and say how sorry I am not to see them this trip. Perhaps I will be able to drop in again before I return to New York.'

'Yes, do that,' the Marquess said affably. 'Enjoy yourself in Monte Carlo, and I hope you win at the tables.'

'I doubt it,' Craig laughed as he walked away. 'But there are other things to entertain one there besides cards.'

There was an obvious innuendo in his voice, and the gaiety with which he spoke brought a knowing smile to those who were near enough to hear what had been said.

Then Craig walked jauntily down the corridor to where his carriage was waiting for him in the street outside.

． ． ． ． ． ． ．

*   *   *

22

The next day Craig Vandervelt left Victoria on the boat-train to Dover.

He travelled with a Courier, two valets, a secretary, and an entire coach was engaged for him and his staff.

At Dover two cabins on the boat were reserved for him and his *entourage* and again there was a private coach reserved for him on the Calais-Mediterranean Express.

As was usual, his secretary provided him with every newspaper and magazine that was published, and there was also a hamper consisting of his favourite drinks and several dishes prepared by his cousin's Chef at Newcastle House.

Craig sat alone thinking out what he had learned from the Marquess and finding the prospect in front of him intriguing and stimulating.

It was nearly a year since he had last undertaken a mission at the request of the Marquess, and although he had known it would be a great mistake to become involved again too soon in Foreign Affairs, and that it was wise that people should forget his existence in that sphere before he appeared again in a world that was very different from his own, he had begun to find that time lay heavy on his hand.

He was growing more cynical than ever about the society which welcomed him in London, Paris and New York.

He knew he owed his entree into every Capital to his father's wealth. At the same time, because he had had such a cosmopolitan education, the social world opened their arms to him and considered him as one of them wherever he went.

Even the most disdainful French aristocrats offered him their hospitality, and although it might originate from the fact that the French respected the fact that his grandfather was a Duke, they soon found that his charm, his almost perfect knowledge of their language, and the fact that he was extremely proficient at their sports all combined to make him a real friend.

He was invited not only to Balls and Receptions in Paris, which were normally exclusively French, but also to go boar-hunting, to shoot and to sail with the young French aristocrats who usually preferred to bar outsiders from their pastimes.

Where women were concerned, the French were no

different from the English or the Americans. They had only to see Craig to behave as if he was the Pied Piper, who must willy-nilly be followed.

Sometimes he told himself it was the golden coins which attracted them, but he would have been very obtuse if he had not realised that they also found him fascinating as a man, and unique as an ardent lover.

'*Jet'adore!*' the French women murmured against his lips, and it was a refrain which was repeated in almost every language from the North to the South Pole.

And yet it was something which Craig himself had never said to a woman.

He could not remember when he had first told himself that he would never say those three words that every woman craved, until they could be spoken not only with his lips, but also with his heart and perhaps, although he was not sure if he had one, his soul.

It was his mother who, because she was so beautiful and he loved her so overwhelmingly, had ingrained in him when he was a child the ideals of chivalry, that love between a man and a woman at its best and its highest was sacred.

Lady Elizabeth, eldest daughter of the Duke of Newcastle, had fallen in love with Cornelius Vandervelt when he came to England as a young man, ambitious, positive, rather aggressively American, and determined to be a millionaire.

He was already rich by European standards, but as far as he himself was concerned, this was only the beginning of the ladder he intended to climb, and no one should stop him from doing so.

He had met Lady Elizabeth in London at a party, and had fallen madly, head-over-heels in love with her.

Like everything else he coveted, he had swept her off her feet and by sheer drive and determination persuaded her to marry him.

It had not been easy, for her father the Duke had been violently opposed to the marriage, but Elizabeth had loved Cornelius in the manner of Romeo and Juliet, Dante and Beatrice, and the Troubadours in the Courts of Love.

24

Theirs had been a blissfully happy marriage until she died when her son was only sixteen.

By that time she had implanted in him her own ideals, her own desire for perfection, and he knew that until he could find a woman as beautiful, as sweet and with the same nobility of character as his mother, he would never be in love.

It was this reserve within him which, because they could not reach the heights he demanded of them, drove women wild.

They had only to meet Craig to fall in love, and almost before he was aware of them would throw themselves and their hearts at his feet.

He would not have been human if he had not accepted the favours that were offered him ever since he had grown up.

At the same time, he became over the years, more and more fastidious, and had grown used to hearing even those he accepted asking:

'What is wrong, Craig? Where have I failed you? What do you expect that I have not given you already?'

It was impossible to explain, impossible to put into words where they did fail him.

Sometimes he would think, when some exquisitely beautiful creature held out her arms to him and her eyes lit up at his approach, that he had found what he was seeking.

But always in a short while he was disappointed, disillusioned, and was back seeking again for what he sensed was just over the horizon, and yet could never reach it.

Of course he had not put all this into words, not even to himself, but sometimes he thought his life was a pilgrimage, and he would never reach the end except in death.

Journeying to Monte Carlo, he was thinking not so much about the Countess Aloya Zladamir as of Randall Sare.

Nobody knew better than he did the importance of his research in Tibet for the British Government.

The son of an explorer who was also an Asiatic scholar, Sare had grown up partly in India and Nepal, and then had been sent to School in England, and to Oxford University.

He had done brilliantly in both, then returned to the land where he had been born and which he loved, to become of inestimable value to the British in what was known as '*The Great Game*'.

All over India there was a secret espionage organisation which recruited men who were trained and initiated in working, and at the same time taking their lives in their hands, for the protection of India and the peace of the Eastern world.

'*The Great Game*' had a network which extended all over India, and involved not only Europeans but a great many Indians as well.

In a locked book in the Indian Survey Department was a list of numbers which represented a variety of secret agents by whom the Russians and enemies of the country were often rendered powerless or exposed when they least expected it.

Randall Sare became an anonymous number in '*The Great Game*' in which his brilliance brought him to the top of the list for those who understood the spider's web which hid such vital secrets.

To Craig it seemed incredible that Sare should first of all have returned from Tibet without anyone in the Foreign Office knowing of it, and secondly that he should have stopped at Monte Carlo, and again not communicated with the English agents there, who should have been known to him.

He began to suspect, as the Marquess had, that he had a good reason for keeping out of sight, which suggested he was being followed and his life was in danger.

Because he not only admired Randall Sare but also liked him as a man, he could only pray that he would be successful where the others had failed and find him as quickly as possible.

He did not underestimate how difficult it would be, and the risk that if he blundered into something which did not concern him, he might endanger both Randall Sare's life and his own.

It was only when he had thought for a long time about a man who knew Tibet perhaps better than any other white man and whose secrets would be a prize beyond price if they fell into the hands of the Russians, that he allowed himself to consider the second mission he had been given – the Countess Aloya Zladamir.

Here again he suspected, as the Marquess did, that if she was

26

pursuing Lord Neasdon there was a good reason for it. At the same time, he could not believe that Neasdon would be so stupid as not to realise in his position how careful he should be in choosing those with whom he associated.

'Russians! Always Russians!' Craig thought to himself.

At the same time, he remembered with satisfaction that there were a number in Monte Carlo with whom he was friendly.

The Archdukes who were enormously wealthy, and most of them extremely attractive, had made Monte Carlo a special haven when they became bored with the pomp of their own country, and the troubles that seemed to increase in the reign of every Tsar.

Once a year they would gravitate like migrating birds towards Monte Carlo where they built themselves magnificently ornate Villas, pursued the most beautiful women, whom they hung with emeralds and pearls, and gambled with astronomical sums in the Casino to the immense satisfaction of the authorities.

There was no race of men who could be more extravagant, more flamboyant, and at the same time more attractive.

Craig looked forward to renewing his acquaintance with the Grand Duke Boris and the Grand Duke Michael, besides being certain that in their circle would be the most alluring and exotic women to be found anywhere in Europe.

He wondered if the Countess Aloya would be amongst them, then some instinct, he was not certain why, told him it was unlikely.

. . . .

As the train puffed early in the morning into Nice, Craig wondered for a moment if he should leave it there and seek his yacht which he had ordered to come from Marseilles to Monte Carlo.

He was certain it would only just have had time to reach Villefranche and it might be more enjoyable to go by sea to the Harbour to Monte Carlo, rather than do the rest of the journey by train.

Then he told himself that would take time, and as it was he

could be in Monte Carlo in another hour.

He therefore stayed on the train, and although his secretary came to his compartment to ask if there was anything he wanted, he merely told him to buy the French morning newspapers and perused them until the line came to an end at the station of Monte Carlo.

From there he walked outside to where an open carriage was waiting for him, leaving his servants to cope with the luggage and follow in another carriage.

He drove off alone, taking off his hat as he did so to feel the sea breeze and the warmth of the sun on his forehead after the heat and stuffiness of the train.

As the horses went down a small incline towards the harbour, he saw a large number of yachts at anchor, some large, some small, all flying the flags of their own countries.

Craig's eyes went from a large number of French flags of red, white and blue, to the White Ensign of the British ships. Then he was aware there were two Russian yachts, side by side, both of them carrying the Imperial Eagle on their flags.

He thought the first thing he would do would be to find out to whom they belonged.

As the horses started to climb the steep hill towards the gold-domed Casino ahead he looked back almost as if the Russian ships drew him like a magnet and they held the secrets that he was seeking to solve.

When Craig Vandervelt stayed in Monte Carlo, being a bachelor he did not rent a Villa which would have been quite easy for him to do, but preferred to stay at the *Hôtel de Paris* and also to have his own yacht in the harbour.

This meant that he was not restricted in any way from leaving at a moment's notice, or, if he wished to be alone or with some very attractive Siren, he could steam along the coast of Italy for a day or two and return when it suited him.

At the *Hôtel de Paris* he was greeted with great respect and the Manager personally took him up to his Suite.

It was very palatial. Not only was it the best in the whole building, but because he liked quiet and privacy Craig usually engaged several rooms on each side of it.

His Sitting-Room was filled with flowers, which might seem unusual for a man, but he not only liked their fragrance but disliked the unlived-in look of Hotel rooms.

There were flowers also in his bedroom and as he looked out of the window he saw his yacht arrive in the harbour below him.

Its lines not only looked beautiful, but the inside of the vessel incorporated every comfort known to those who sailed the seas.

Craig Vandervelt's mind was never still, and he had invented a number of gadgets, some of which had already been adopted by other yacht-owners while some were so new that no one else had as yet, become aware of them.

He thought with satisfaction that he would be able to test some of his most recent innovations in the next few days, but at the moment the most important thing was to find his bearings and take the first step in his plan to discover Randall Sare.

Nobody seeing him half-an-hour later, however, sauntering out into the sunshine would have suspected that Craig was thinking of anything except his own enjoyment of the frivolities of the small Principality of Monaco.

Already, although it was still early, many of the more important guests were taking the air, walking along the terraced garden behind the Casino or across the Square towards the tables outside the *Café de la Paix* where the gossips sat drinking *aperitifs* and criticising each other.

Almost before he had gone a few steps Craig was greeted by friends and acquaintances.

'Craig! I was sure you would be here!' one lovely woman wrapped in sables and wearing a King's ransom in jewels, exclaimed.

And Gaby Delys, the most talked-of and acclaimed actress in Paris, wearing a hat covered in ospreys, kissed him on both cheeks.

'*Mon cher* Craig! I am enchanted to see you!'

Craig bowed, kissed the soft hands, and moved as the morning progressed, from one table to another, from one group to the next.

He was always sure of his welcome, always certain that there would be an invitation in the sparkling eyes of the women who saw him and a provocative pout to their red lips.

When finally he had ordered himself a very small *aperitif* and was seated beside Zsi-Zsi de la Tour, who was a notorious gossip, he asked:

'Tell me, Zsi-Zsi, who is in Monte Carlo?'

'As far as I am concerned, *mon brave*, there is only you!'

Craig twisted his lips.

'What would the Grand Duke say to that?'

She shrugged her shoulders in a typically French manner.

'He will be jealous, which is good for him!'

Craig laughed.

'I have no desire to disrupt His Imperial Highness's happy time with you.'

'Which is a polite way of saying in English you have "other fish to fry",' Zsi-Zsi answered.

Craig laughed.

Zsi-Zsi was always unpredictable, and although the fiery love-affair they had had together was over five years ago, they had remained friends and he would never have thought of going to Paris without visiting her.

Craig looked round.

'I see very few new faces and quite a lot of them have grown older.'

'That is definitely unkind of you, Craig, and not like the pretty speeches you used to make.'

'I am not referring to you,' Craig protested. 'You know as well as I do, that you are eternally young, and more beautiful with every year that passes.'

'That is better!' Zsi-Zsi approved, 'and I only wish it were true. However Boris at least still finds me irresistible.'

'I am glad about that. I like him, and I see he has given you some very pretty baubles.'

Craig looked mockingly as he spoke at the huge emeralds that encircled Zsi-Zsi's neck, and the one that was almost the size of a *louis* on her finger.

She gave him a provocative little glance from under her mascaraed eye-lashes before she said:

'Do you know which one I treasure most of all the jewels I have been given?'

'I have no idea.'

'The little St. Christopher you gave me and you may believe me when I tell you that I always carry it in my bag. It is my luck, my talisman, and inevitably a *bon chance* in the Casino.'

'I am glad,' Craig smiled, 'and now I return to my original question. Who is here with whom I can amuse myself, since you are definitely *engagée*?'

'Now let me think. . .' Zsi-Zsi pondered. 'I understand you would not wish as the English say to "boil your vegetables in the same water twice".'

'Certainly not.'

Zsi-Zsi pursed her lips together.

'Now I think about it there are very few new faces!' she paused, then she added: 'There is one, but I have no idea from where she comes.'

'Who is that?' Craig asked in a voice of indifference, his eyes moving over the crowd drinking and talking around them.

'She calls herself,' Zsi-Zsi replied, 'the Countess Aloya Zladamir, but Boris says he has never heard of her.'

CHAPTER TWO

When Craig returned to the *Hôtel de Paris* he went first to the Reception Desk to ask if there were any letters for him.

While the man was looking he glanced quickly at the Hotel Register which stood open on the counter.

He had long ago taught himself to read upside-down, and among a long list of celebrities he saw the name for which he was looking.

It was a great satisfaction to know that the Countess was under the same roof, and when the man returned to hand him several letters bearing American stamps, Craig said casually:

'I am pleased with my rooms, but I hope you have not placed a lot of noisy people on my floor, as you did two years ago.'

'I am sure, *Monsieur* Vandervelt, you will find it very quiet,' the Receptionist answered quickly.

'I hope you are right,' Craig said with a doubtful note in his voice.

The Receptionist looked at the keys behind him.

'One of the guests near you, *Monsieur*, is the Duke of Norfolk, who always retires to bed early, and another is the Grand Duke of Lichtenstein.'

Craig nodded as if he was more or less satisfied, then as if he was anxious to please him the Receptionist added:

'Another is the Countess Aloya Zladamir, a newcomer to the *Hôtel de Paris*.'

'I do not think I have heard of her,' Craig said casually, and walked away with an air of indifference.

He had however discovered what he wanted to know, and

asking more or less the same question of the waiter who brought him some *Evian* water he learned that the Countess's room adjoined the last one which was a part of his own Suite.

This meant that the balcony of her Sitting-Room looked out in the same direction as his, at the magnificent view of the sea, the harbour and the Palace perched high on the promontory.

Craig already had an invitation to luncheon, and as he went downstairs he found his friends drinking in the ante-room of the Restaurant and wondered if he would see the Countess, and if he would be able to recognise her.

He had known a number of Russian women who were exceedingly beautiful, and he thought they usually had a flamboyance about them which appealed, as their male counterparts did, to the romantic notions which the rest of the world had about the Russians.

It might be true of the aristocrats, but no one knew better than Craig how completely ruthless and often brutal the Russian soldiers were in Afghanistan and in other countries under their control.

In the crowded Restaurant, with its painted walls, crystal chandeliers and gold ornamentation, were a great number of people he knew and who greeted him with varying degrees of delight, but there was no one who, he thought, was likely to be the Countess.

He also saw Lord Neasdon lunching with two gentlemen of about the same age as himself, but without any female companion.

When luncheon was over, Craig with some difficulty disentangled himself from his friends, and saying he needed the exercise walked from the *Hôtel de Paris* down the hill in the direction of the harbour.

He knew that by this time his yacht had arrived, but he had another mission on the way, which took him, surprisingly enough, to the small Church under the railway arch where few of the gambling visitors to Monte Carlo were ever seen.

The Chapel to St. Devoté had been built at the foot of a deep ravine so that little light penetrated through the stained-glass windows, and inside it was dark, save for the candles flickering in front of a statue.

There were only two old women with shawls over their heads kneeling in prayer as Craig entered, and he moved softly up the side aisle to where there was a Confessional Box.

He entered it, and was aware that there was a Priest on the other side of an open grating.

They could not see each other, but the Priest obviously sensed his presence and after a moment said in Latin:

*'In nomine Patris et Filii, et Spiritus Sancti, Amen.'

Craig knelt so that his face was near to the grating, and he said in a low voice that it would have been impossible for anybody outside to hear:

'Is that you, Father Augustin? This is Craig.'

There was a silence of surprise before the Priest said:
'I had not heard, *Mon fils*, that you had arrived.'

'I only got into Monte Carlo a few hours ago.'

'It is agreeable to know that you are back with us again.'

'I am glad to be here, but Father, I need your help.'

There was a faint note of amusement in the Priest's voice as he answered:

'I might have guessed that would be the reason for such an immediate visit.'

'I am searching for somebody,' Craig said, 'who is, I believe, in great danger.'

'And you think I may know of him?'

'I have no other way of contacting him, and you, Father, have helped me in the past to prevent a man losing his life, which is a gift from God.'

'Tell me the name of the man you seek.'

'Randall Sare.'

'Should I have heard of him?'

'You may have done. His father, Conrad Sare, was a great Oriental Scholar whose books are read all over the world by those who would learn from the East. I am sure most Monastery Libraries contain his work on Buddhism.'

*'In the name of the Father and of the Son and of the Holy Ghost. Amen.'

The Priest gave a low exclamation.

'Now I know of whom you speak. It is his son you are looking for?'

'I know he was in Monte Carlo a few weeks ago, but I think he is now hiding from men who are pursuing him.'

'Where did he come from?'

Just for a moment Craig hesitated. Then knowing that he could trust the man to whom he was speaking, he said quietly:

'From Tibet.'

He knew there was no need to say any more. Father Augustin was extremely intelligent and, as Craig had found in the past, well-informed.

There was a pause before he said:

'I will do what I can.'

'That is all I ask,' Craig said, 'and thank you, Father. I am quite certain you have a large number of poor who need the solace of a few American dollars.'

'Do not thank me until I have been able to help you,' the Priest answered, 'and come, if you can, again tomorrow.'

'I will do that, and thank you, *Mon Père*. I would like you to know that the last man you helped is living comfortably outside New York and is very content to be an American citizen.'

'I will thank God for His help in enabling me to rescue him,' the Priest said quietly.

Craig rose from his knees.

'Goodbye Father, and I cannot tell you how grateful I am for your help.'

In a voice that carried beyond the thin walls of the Confessional the Priest said:

*'Misereatur vestri omnipoteus Deus, et dimissis peccatis vestris perducat vos ad vitam aeternam.'

As Craig parted the curtain and went back into the Church he saw there was only one elderly woman waiting to take his place at the Confessional Box and she did not even raise her eyes as he passed.

'May Almighty God have mercy upon you, forgive you your sins and bring you to life everlasting.'

At the same time, he knew that he could not be too careful and as he reached the statue of Joan of Arc he lit a candle and dropped a few coins noisily into the box in front of it.

Then he walked out into the sunshine feeling as if he had transferred some of his problem onto shoulders that were broader than his own.

Nobody who knew Craig would have expected him to be friends with a Catholic Priest, and as he walked quickly to the road leading directly to the harbour he hoped he would not be noticed.

There was however little likelihood of that since at this time of day the visitors to Monte Carlo were either sleeping off the very large luncheon they had eaten, or already were finding their fingers itching for the cards in the exclusive *Salle Touzet*.

The main Casino, to which the *Salle Touzet* was a recent addition, would be filled by the ordinary people of the town, and the unimportant visitors, hypnotised by the rolling balls of the Roulette tables, and Craig was glad that he had no reason to join them.

He reached the harbour and found as he expected that his yacht was already moored, and the gang-plank was down on the quay.

He walked aboard to be greeted by his Captain and First Officer, who were obviously genuinely delighted that they had been ordered to put to sea after spending the winter in harbour at Marseilles.

'Where do you plan to go, Mr. Vandervelt?' the Captain asked eagerly, and Craig knew he was hoping they would not linger too long in any harbour.

'I do not know for the moment,' he replied, 'but I would like you to be ready to leave at a moment's notice. You know how restless I become when I am confined to one place.'

'That is what I was hoping you would say, Sir,' the Captain replied. 'The Greek islands are very attractive at this time of the year.'

'I had not forgotten that,' Craig agreed, then added in a more practical tone: 'Are all the new gadgets I ordered installed?'

36

'Aye, aye, Sir, and I hope you will come and see them.'

Craig started with the bridge and saw some of his inventions in action, then walked round the yacht noting that the pictures he had ordered had been hung, a new idea for keeping the tables steady in a storm had been installed, and that the very much larger bed he had bought for his State-Room because he found the last one too cramped, was in place.

It was only when he went back on deck again that he said:

'I see there are two Russian yachts in the harbour. Will you find out to whom they belong?'

'I have already asked that, Sir,' the Captain answered, 'but when I enquired I could not obtain an answer. The Duke of Westminster's yacht however is magnificent, and Mr. Pierpont Morgan is aboard his, which arrived here I am told, last week.'

Craig was listening and he was also noting that there was a mooring between the Duke of Westminister's and the first of the Russian yachts.

After a moment he said:

'As I am rather interested to see if the Russians are as advanced as we are ourselves, I think it might be a good idea if we go out to sea for the next hour and when we return, move into the mooring next to the first yacht carrying the Imperial Flag.'

'I am sure that can be arranged, Sir,' the Captain replied. 'I will just go and have a word with the Harbour Master.'

The Captain went ashore and Craig spent the time on a further inspection of his yacht.

She was named 'The Mermaid' and he had supervised every inch of her while she was being built. He thought in fact, he would be very piqued if any of the other expensive and magnificent–looking yachts in the harbour had any more advanced technology than his, or were in any way more comfortable.

He did not have to wait long before the Captain returned, and he knew before the man spoke that his request had been refused.

'I am sorry, Mr. Vandervelt,' he said, 'but the Harbour Master tells me that the Russians are not at the moment using that particular mooring but have reserved and paid for it.'

Craig raised his eye-brows, but he did not say anything and the Captain went on:

'It seems extraordinary and rather high-handed, but the Harbour Master told me that all the best places which are those straight onto the Quay are fully booked, and he had already had three requests this morning which he has had to turn down and offer the applicants a mooring out in the harbour.'

Because this meant being rowed ashore every time one left the yacht, Craig knew that most owners found it extremely irritating.

Now with a smile he said:

'Well, we should be thankful you were clever enough to get this place. Now show me what speed *'The Mermaid'* can do with her new engine.'

Two hours later when Craig left the yacht he again walked up the hill towards the Casino.

He had his own car in Monte Carlo although he had not yet asked for it, and he was aware that his chauffeur would not only be wanting to see him, but would also be anxious to enquire if he would enter in the *Concours d'Élégance* which had been inaugurated two years ago and proved a tremendous success.

This thought gave Craig an idea, as he remembered that those who owned their own cars would be looking for a beautiful lady to show off.

He had taken part in this *Concours* the previous year and remembered that the motor cars were exhibited on the terrace below the Casino, where they were examined by a Jury.

At 3 p.m. they went in procession around the gardens, then pulled up in front of a grand-stand where the prizes were awarded. After this they circled the gardens again and further prizes were given to the most elegantly dressed woman in a car.

Last year, Craig had taken the *Grand Prix d'Honneur* as the

38

chief award. Although the policy was never to give second or third prizes the announcements gave not only the names of those who were first in the *Prix d'Honneur*, the *Grand Prix d'Honneur*, and the *Premier Prix*, but also the names of the ladies, their dressmakers and milliners.

This ensured frantic competition both amongst the ladies themselves and those who dressed them.

Craig remembered with amusement that the very alluring beauty who won the prize with him had told him that this ensured that she would be dressed by her Parisian dressmaker for the rest of the year, in gowns which would be either free or at half price.

Because he was looking for somebody spectacular who he was certain he would recognise on sight, he walked into the Casino and through the ordinary gaming rooms into the *Salle Touzet*.

There were lovely, elegantly dressed and beautiful women at almost every table, their eyes glued to the cards or the Roulette wheel, and therefore paying little attention either to the men who sat beside them or to those who wandered about looking for somebody to entertain them.

Craig found the Grand Duke Boris smoking a last cigar while Zsi-Zsi was for the moment intent only on staking the gold *louis* he had given her on what she considered her 'lucky numbers'.

Craig was well aware how superstitious Zsi-Zsi was, but that was nothing new, for every gambler had what they believed was a lucky charm which would ensure their winning at the tables.

He had known women who carried with them the skin of a venomous snake, an eagle's claw, a rabbit's foot and even a piece of a hangman's rope.

He had also known men who put a spoonful of salt in the pockets of their evening-coats to induce the cards to bring them luck.

He had always thought them ridiculous, since all a man really wanted was an intuition which warned him of danger, and a perception which told him there was trouble ahead.

However this was something he would not have said to the Grand Duke Boris who, like most of his countrymen, believed that luck was a lady and could therefore be wooed.

'How are you, Craig?' the Grand Duke asked genially.

'All the better for seeing you, Sir,' Craig replied. 'Are you enjoying yourself?'

'Things seem to be pretty dull at the moment,' the Grand Duke replied. 'But I must certainly give a party now that you have arrived. What about tomorrow night?'

'I shall be very honoured,' Craig replied.

'I will tell Zsi-Zsi to ask all your particular friends, but none of your enemies, if you have any.'

'I am always hoping they are few and far between.'

'There you are right,' the Grand Duke said. 'You are a very popular man, Craig, and as I understand you are alone we must find somebody who is beautiful to keep you anchored here for at least a little while.'

He paused before he added:

'I see that your yacht is in the harbour so that you will be able to steal away without our being able to prevent you.'

Craig laughed.

'I have every intention of staying for a while. I find New York boring, and I have no wish to be in London at this time of the year.'

'I expect it is raining.'

'I am sure it is,' Craig laughed.

As they were talking they had moved across the room to where there was an open window and sat down at a table in the centre of it.

A waiter came hurrying to the Grand Duke's side.

He ordered a bottle of champagne then said to Craig as if it was on his mind:

'There is one damned pretty woman I have not seen before, but she seems to be caught up with one of your countrymen. I expect you know him – Lord Neasdon?'

'Actually I have never met him,' Craig replied. 'What is he like?'

'Pompous, and I find it strange that anything so attractive

as the Countess Aloya Zladamir should find him interesting.'

Craig did not answer for a moment. Then he said:

'With a name like that I suppose she is one of your countrymen?'

I suppose so,' the Grand Duke said. 'I have never met any Zladamirs, but that is not to say that they do not exist.'

Craig laughed.

'You could not be expected to know everybody in a country the size of yours.'

'She is also very young,' the Grand Duke continued as if he was following the train of his own thoughts, 'and I cannot make up my mind whether she belongs to the *Monde* or the *demi-Monde*.'

'Surely that is not a very difficult decision at least for somebody as discriminating as Your Imperial Highness.'

'I have an idea that you are "pulling my leg",' the Grand Duke said, 'but I admit this woman has me baffled. I got myself introduced to her and believe it or not, she made it very clear that she was not interested in me!'

The Grand Duke spoke in an ingenuous way which made Craig want to laugh.

He was well aware that to know the Grand Duke Boris, handsome, rich and exceedingly generous with a flamboyant personality which dominated the social scene of Monte Carlo, was the ambition of every woman whether she belonged to the *Beau Monde* or the *demi-Monde*.

In fact Craig was certain that if what the Grand Duke had said was true it was the first time he had ever shown an interest in a woman of any social class and had not been responded to with enthusiasm.

What had happened had obviously piqued him, for he continued:

'I should have thought being here alone in Monte Carlo for the first time she would have jumped at the opportunity of extending her acquaintances. But no! She is seen either with Neasdon or alone.'

'A possible explanation is that she is in love with him.'

'I do not believe it!' the Grand Duke replied. 'He may be a

very good Diplomat, but I am quite certain he is as much of a bore in bed as he is at the dinner-table!'

Craig laughed again.

'That is certainly condemning, especially when it is the opinion of an expert like yourself, Sir.'

The Grand Duke had the grace to laugh as well.

'I am probably making a fuss about nothing, Craig,' he said. 'At the same time it really annoyed me. But do not say anything to Zsi-Zsi. She of course has no idea that I approached this woman.'

'You know that anything you say to me is in confidence.'

'Well, I shall try asking her to the party tomorrow night, and you can have a look at her,' the Grand Duke said a little heavily as he sipped the champagne which had just been poured out for him. 'But I doubt if she will come.'

'Why not try asking Neasdon and suggest that he brings her with him?'

The Grand Duke chuckled.

'I might have known you would have a solution to the knotty problem! But of course! That is the ticket! And Neasdon, I should imagine, will be quite pleased to be invited to one of my parties. I have never sent him an invitation before.'

'I am sure he would be delighted, Sir, and make quite sure the invitation is a dual one.'

'I will!' the Grand Duke agreed firmly.

They talked of the *Concours d'Élégance* and the Grand Duke had invited himself aboard *'The Mermaid'* before Craig left him.

As he walked back to the Hôtel de Paris he felt he had done a good day's work, although he had not actually made contact with the two people with whom he was most concerned.

Then as he walked along the corridor to his own Suite he saw in front of him a very elegant figure.

His first impression was of a woman moving with a grace that was unusual and she was also exceedingly slim.

Then as he stopped at his own door and she turned in at a door at the far end of the corridor, he realised he had seen the back view of the Countess Aloya Zladimir.

As he entered his own Suite he thought again what a lucky coincidence it was that she should have rooms connecting with his, and that actually the room next to hers was empty.

'My luck has not failed me,' Craig told himself. 'I have no need of snakes, hangmen's ropes, or black cats!'

He read the newspapers until it was time to dress for dinner and when he had changed into the smart, close-fitting tail-coat which, like all his other clothes was made in London's Savile Row, he went downstairs to find the party with whom he was dining.

They were old friends he had encountered on the terrace in front of the Casino this morning, and they had insisted on his joining him, and he was only too willing to do so.

He was already making a list in his mind of the people with whom he wished to renew his acquaintance, and those he wished to avoid.

The Prince and Princess of Braganza who were his hosts this evening were charming, and she was very attractive.

They were only a party of ten and were seated at one of the best tables at the side of the room where the windows overlooked the garden in front of the Casino which was brilliant with fairy-lights.

There were also fairy-lights in the trees, and with the stars coming out and a pale moon shining its light on the dome of the Casino the whole place looked enchanted.

The guests in the Dining-Room of the *Hôtel de Paris* looked enchanted too, and Craig wondered if anywhere else in the world one could find in one place, more beautiful women or more handsome, aristocratic men, all the finest representatives of their different nations.

The conversation from the moment they sat down at the table was sparkling, and Craig found himself talking in first one language, then another, and contriving in his own inimitable way to be witty in them all.

Everybody was laughing, and it seemed as if a crescendo of voices was rising from all the other tables, when suddenly by the door there seemed to be a sudden hush, which spread

43

gradually over the room.

Craig looked round, saw the reason, and was not surprised.

Moving into the Dining Room was the most beautiful and unusual woman he had ever seen and as he looked at her and saw who walked behind her he knew who she was.

One man at the table murmured:

'By Jove! That is something to look at!' and Craig thought he could have echoed his words.

She was, as he had noticed when he had seen her walking down the passage, very slim. She was also taller than many other women in the room, and if she had dressed in order to cause a sensation she had certainly succeeded.

Every other woman was clothed in colours of the spring fashions: green, blue, pink, yellow, and a great deal of soft white chiffon or tulle.

The Countess Aloya was wearing black. It was quite a severe black and the bodice was plain and very tight, accentuating the soft curves of her breasts and her very small waist.

Her skirts, billowing out, were not ornamented, and what at first glance seemed so extraordinary was that unlike every other woman in the room she was not glittering with jewels.

Craig as a connoisseur of women knew there was no need for them, for the whiteness of her skin was a jewel in itself, and her hair, so fair that it seemed almost silver in the light from the chandeliers, appeared to glitter without the aid of diamonds.

Only when she had drawn nearer to a table not far from Craig was he able to see that on one side of her bodice was pinned a brooch with one enormous stone the same colour as her hair and he knew it was a yellow diamond.

She was spectacular but, far more important, she was really beautiful. Her eyes were enormous, slanting up a little at the corners, and her eyelashes very dark.

Although he could not see the colour of her eyes he suspected, because she was Russian, they would be green.

Without that coloured hair she could easily have belonged to another nationality, though for the moment he could not

44

think what it might be.

Almost as if he was a Producer of a Play, the *Maître d'Hôtel* ushered the Countess to a table for two which was next to the one occupied by Craig's party.

The Countess sat down facing him and now he could see the exquisite symmetry of her small straight nose, and that her lips were softly curved and strangely, he thought, gave the impression, although of course it was ridiculous, of being a little unsure and apprehensive.

Then he told himself he was imagining things, and yet he knew he was looking at a face that was so different, and so unusual that it was hard to find words to describe it even to himself.

For the moment all the conversation at the table at which he was sitting had ceased. Then his hostess the Princess said:

'I must admit, she is surprising! Last night she wore dead white that was almost like a Grecian gown, and her only jewel was a pearl ring the size of a pigeon's egg.'

'Have you met her?' Craig enquired.

The Princess smiled and shook her head.

'My husband has not yet made up his mind whether it is *comme il faut* for me to do so.'

Craig laughed.

'The Grand Duke is just as undecided as you are,' he said. 'But surely this is a very unusual enigma in Monte Carlo of all places?'

'Very, very unusual,' the Princess agreed, 'but I assure you, every man in the place is trying to discover the secret of the Sphinx, and every women, including myself, is hoping they will not do so too quickly.'

Craig laughed again.

As the conversation returned to normal, however, he found it hard to take his eyes from the woman sitting almost opposite to him.

Although he could not hear what she said, he knew that Lord Neasdon was droning on with a monologue which he was quite sure was very boring.

His companion appeared to be listening attentively, and,

Craig supposed, encouragingly.

At the same time, she was certainly not being in the least flirtatious nor did she appear to be enticing him with glances or provocative pouts of her lips as almost every other woman in the room was doing.

He looked around and saw *La Belle Otero*, one of the most famous Courtesans in the whole of Paris, making the men with whom she dined, sit spellbound as she talked to them.

They raised their glasses again and again to drink her health, and undoubtedly promised that sooner or later they would add to her famous and priceless collection of jewels.

When he had first seen her, Craig had thought it was impossible for any woman to be more alluring, and he had not been surprised when he had learned that the cupolas on the corners of the new Carlton Hotel at Cannes were shaped to resemble *La Belle's* breasts.

At another table there was *La Juniory*, who had had a bed made in the shape of an enormous conch shell, and *Gaby Delys*, the toast of Paris, whom he had seen earlier in the day and who was as usual festooned in pearls, each string longer and more valuable than the last.

But all these women paled beside the beauty of the Countess Aloya and Craig found himself wondering what there was about her that made her unique.

He told himself after studying her for some time that it was not only her features, her unusual eyes, or her hair which she swept back in the elegant, but simple style made famous by Dana Gibson.

There was, he thought perceptively, something deeper, something that emanated from her almost as if she was surrounded by an aura of her own personality.

Anyway, as far as he was concerned, she was as brilliant as if she was enveloped in light.

It might be, he told himself scornfully, that he was intrigued because of what the Marquess of Lansdowne had said, yet he found it difficult all through the long meal that followed to take his eyes from the woman at the next table.

He was determined to meet her, and he thought it was far

46

too long to wait until the next evening to find out if Neasdon had taken the bait offered to him by the Grand Duke, and would bring her to the party at his Villa.

But try as he could, when they all went onto the Casino he found it impossible to find anyone who could introduce him to the unknown Countess.

He thought of walking up to Neasdon and saying that the Marquess of Lansdowne had told him they would meet in Monte Carlo and introducing himself. But that was something he had no wish to do.

But he could not think of any other way of talking either to Lord Neasdon or to his companion.

They were in the *Salle Touzet* at the Casino, but Neasdon did not gamble nor did she.

Instead they sat at one of the tables talking to each other or drinking champagne but, although Lord Neasdon had obviously a great deal to say and took a long time in doing so, neither of them seemed particularly animated.

As Craig moved around the room talking to friends, pretending to watch what numbers came up on the Roulette Tables, or standing behind those who were playing Baccaret, he thought he had never been so frustrated or so helpless.

In the past every social problem had seemed far easier. In fact he could never remember wanting to get to know somebody, especially a woman, without it happening almost before he thought of it.

Although he went very near to the Countess at times, he was aware she never once raised her eyes to look up at him or any other of the people in the room.

She merely appeared to be listening attentively to Lord Neasdon, occasionally speaking to him, sometimes making a gesture with her left hand.

'What can I do?' Craig asked himself, and felt like swearing when half an hour after midnight he saw the Countess rise to her feet.

Lord Neasdon obviously expostulated with her, doubtless begging her not to retire so early, but she moved insistently towards the door and Craig unobtrusively followed.

She obtained a black velvet cape from the Cloakroom Woman, placed it round her shoulders and walked ahead towards the door.

Again, because he could not help himself, Craig followed, and as she went down the steps and out into the moonlight he saw her raise her face up towards the sky.

He saw the long line of her white neck, and he thought, although he could not be sure, that she wished upon a star, as women have done since the beginning of time.

Then with Lord Neasdon still muttering, she walked quickly towards the lights of the *Hôtel de Paris* and disappeared up the steps through the door into the Reception Lounge.

Craig, without even thinking that he should have said goodnight to his host and hostess, walked after her at a discreet distance.

By the time he had reached his own floor, he was not surprised, although he thought he should have been, to see the Countess walking alone ahead of him as she had done earlier in the day.

Even as he went into his own Suite he heard her door close decisively.

It was then he told himself that whatever her association with Lord Neasdon might be, he was not her lover and, what was more, it was unlikely that he would join her later.

Craig felt sure of this because he had sent his Valet downstairs to find out if Lord Neasdon was staying in the Hotel.

The Valet had returned with the information that His Lordship was in fact at *'L'Hermitage'* which was a little higher up the town, and the next most important Hotel in Monte Carlo.

In his own Suite, Craig stood for a moment thinking.

Then as if his instinct told him what to do he walked through the communicating door of his Sitting Room into his bedroom and opened another almost identical door which led into the empty room which communicated with that of the Countess.

He was well aware that the door, both on his side and hers had been locked by the staff, and would only be opened if they asked for the key.

Again following his instinct he opened first the window, then the shutters and went out onto the balcony.

The spring air was cool as he moved out and the vista below, with the lights in the yachts in the harbour and on the promontory above, was very beautiful.

The stars were reflecting in the sea and the white light of the moon turned everything to silver, which made him think of the Countess's hair.

Then as he thought of her he heard her come out onto the next balcony and as she did so she sighed.

She obviously had no idea that he was there. She had taken off her cloak and the moonlight was on the whiteness of her neck and arms, and the silver of her hair.

She stood at the front of the balcony with her hands on the stone balustrade, and once again as she looked up at the stars Craig had the strange feeling that she was praying.

She stood there for some minutes. Then he said very quietly and softly:

'I have always thought that this is one of the most beautiful views in the world.'

She started as he spoke, and turned her face to look at him, then quickly away again.

He did not say any more, but almost as if he compelled her to answer him she said after a moment in a voice that he thought trembled:

'I . . I did not know that . . you were . . there!'

'I only arrived today.'

There was silence. Then he said:

'I always feel as if those yachts below us are straining at their moorings, longing to leave in search of adventure which lies somewhere beyond the horizon.'

He spoke in the voice he might have used to a child when telling a fairy-story, and almost as if she entered into the fantasy she replied:

'That is what I would love to do, to sail away and . . never come back!'

49

'Do you mean to this world, or to Monte Carlo in particular?'

'To Monte . . Carlo.'

He had a feeling because her voice was different from the way she had spoken before that her answer was personal and impulsive.

Then as if she regretted what she had said she added:

'I must go in. I am told the nights here can be very . . treacherous.'

'That is true,' Craig replied, 'but actually the temperature today has been very mild, and unless you feel cold, I do not think you will come to any harm.'

'I hope not!'

As she spoke, once again Craig's perception told him she was not thinking of herself.

Almost as if the words were put into his mind he said:

'Of course with the elderly it is always wise to take precautions in this climate which can be very changeable. They should be well wrapped up at night and remember that the wind that comes from the Alps can definitely be treacherous.'

There was then no doubt that she drew in her breath sharply and she said as if she spoke to herself:

'If that is true, then one should be very, very careful if one has come from a hot climate.'

'Of course,' Craig agreed, 'I remember once when I returned from India and stopped at Monte Carlo that I was laid up for several days, entirely through my own fault.'

'You have been to India?'

'Several times.' he answered, 'It is a country with which I have a deep affinity.'

There was silence. Then the Countess said:

'I am sure if you have . . once been there you could never . . forget it.'

'Of course not,' Craig agreed, 'and when I am in India I think how foolish we are not to listen to what it has to say.'

She turned her face towards him and he knew that for a second she looked at him in surprise. Then she looked away again to say:

'In the West . . everything is very . . different.'

50

'Yes, but that is not to say that we know more or are any better as human beings.'

Again there was silence before she asked almost as if she could not help herself:

'Where have you . . been in India?'

Craig gave a little laugh.

'It would be almost easier to tell you where I have not been. It is a country of such beauty that it captivates the eye, and also, as I expect you know, holds the mind spellbound. From the moment one steps onto Indian soil, one starts to learn, and goes on learning.'

'How do you know, and how can you . . think like . . that?'

'I might ask you the same question,' Craig replied, 'and shall I say that as India has introduced us to each other there is so much I would like to talk to you about.'

The Countess made a little gesture which he felt was one of eagerness. Then suddenly she looked down, he thought, into the harbour, before she said in a voice which he thought trembled:

'I . . I must go to bed . . goodnight, Sir.'

Without waiting for his reply, she turned and left the balcony, closing the window behind her.

Then as he stood without moving, wondering at her haste at leaving him, wondering at the strange tremor in her voice, he heard somebody else speak in her room.

For a moment he thought it was a man.

Then as he listened, not sure, the window was opened and somebody pulled the shutters to and bolted them.

It was a maid, and he knew that it was her voice he had heard, and she had been speaking in Russian.

CHAPTER THREE

The next day Craig was determined to find out more about the Russian yachts in the harbour.

He thought he had not done too badly so far in making contact with the Countess, but though that was fairly satisfactory what he was really concerned about was Randall Sare.

Ever since he had met him in India when he was only twenty-one, Randall Sare had been in his eyes a hero, somebody he admired more than any other man he had ever met.

It was the Viceroy who had first spoken of him in a way which told Craig that there was something special about the man who awoke a look of admiration in a pair of tired eyes and brought to his voice a note which he had recognised as one of respect.

The Viceroy of India had an importance that was incomparable with that of almost any other ruler in the world.

There was no King or Emperor who had more power or who, in a huge country where white men reigned supreme, lived with more pomp and circumstance.

Needless to say, the British took their games with them wherever they went, and sport being their chief spiritual export, the young soldiers, full of dash and energy, spent every moment when they were not on duty enjoying their national games.

It was inevitable that as soon as Craig Vandervelt arrived in India with his aura of wealth glowing around him, he should be taken to Calcutta for the races.

From Calcutta with its race dances, public breakfasts and curious alternations of sweep-stake and country dance, he went on to Simla where the race course on a high plateau of Annandale was surrounded by tall pines and deodars and was deliciously secluded.

Because Craig not only owned with his father the best race horses in America, but was also an outstanding rider, he was accepted automatically as a 'good chap'.

The great day of the Calcutta Year was the day of the Viceroy's Cup Race, the cup being given annually by the reigning Viceroy.

The grandstand was filled with beautiful and important women from England, America – in fact from all parts of the world, and to Craig it had a fascination and delight he had not expected.

Having once been accepted by the British as one of them he was introduced to their hunting which consisted in India of a pack of hounds reinforced with an odd terrier who set off in pursuit of jackal, elk, pig, hare, red deer, hyena, or whatever else was available to chase.

It was after he had proved himself in that field as well as on the race course, and had taken up pig-sticking and Polo, that he found himself dining at Government House and in the Officer's Mess of the most important Regiments.

It was there he first heard a murmur of *'The Great Game'*, only very little, but enough to make him curious.

Because he had a retentive memory as well as an insatiable curiosity he was able to put a remark made after dinner together with some disjointed conversation in a Civil Servant's office, and it began to make a pattern.

It was after the Viceroy had spoken of Randall Sare that he asked a few questions and received somewhat ambiguous answers.

'Randall Sare – strange chap, brilliantly clever, I'm told, but prefers to mix with the natives rather than us.'

At first Craig was naïve enough to think that 'the natives' meant Rajahs and Maharajahs who entertained lavishly in their Palaces, whose hospitality almost any Englishman would accept.

Then he learnt from what somebody else said that Randall Sare in various disguises spoke every language known in India, and frequently vanished for months on end, although where to and why, nobody seemed to be ready to explain.

It was only when being quite by chance in Simla he met the man himself, that he began to understand and to admire him.

Not very tall, Randall Sare had one of those strange, unforgettable faces which was, as it happened, easy to disguise because he did not rely on the make-up that any actor would have used, but on thought, on a lifetime's knowledge of the people among whom he moved and whose personalities he often assumed instead of his own.

Because Craig found it impossible to forget him, he had deliberately sought him out on his second journey to India, and found as he expected that he was one of the most interesting men he had ever met, and a mine of information on all the subjects which no-one else had ever discussed with him.

The Indian castes, the creeds of men who were merely an enigma to the Western Powers were subjects that Craig found irresistible, and which to Randall Sare were the breath of life.

It was then that Craig began to understand how men like Sare could love a country as another man could love a woman.

India was not only a teeming continent which when it had been conquered had to be organised, made respectable and civilised by the social standards of Cheltenham, but there was also a marvellously complex way of life that hid beneath its surface secrets which had inspired some of the greatest religions in the world.

Because at the age of twenty-four Craig was prepared to sit at the feet and become a pupil of a man who he was astute enough to realise was a giant among other men, he learnt from Randall Sare in the short time they were together more than other men learnt or even touched the fringe of in a whole lifetime.

It was three years ago on his third visit to India that Randall

Sare told him he was going to Tibet.

'Why?' Craig had asked bluntly.

'I am convinced,' Randall Sare replied, 'that the Russians are absorbing one after another the Khans of Central Asia, and are aiming to control the whole of the northern frontier of India.'

'It cannot be possible!'

'They are already building a Railway across Siberia to the Far East,' Sare went on, 'and I am told they are also building a Railway in Turkestan, and . .'

He paused for a moment.

'. . planning the annexation of Tibet.'

'I thought no-one was allowed into that country,' Craig remarked.

'I think it would be difficult to stop Russia if they were determined,' Sare replied, 'and if that is what they intend, that is what they will do.'

'How can we prevent it?'

Randall Sare smiled and it gave him an attraction that was all his own.

'That is what I am going to find out.'

When he said goodbye Craig knew it would be a long time before he would see him again, if ever.

Now, if the Marquess was to be believed, Sare had not only returned to Europe, but had disappeared in Monte Carlo.

It seemed incredible first that Sare should leave India without the Foreign Office being informed of it, and secondly that he should have stopped in a place that was known as the most frivolous, extravagant and wicked in the whole of Europe.

Bishops and Clergy of every denomination thundered continually against the wickedness that prevailed in the 'City of gambling'.

Yet the Casino of Monte Carlo was patronised by almost every Crowned Head and the threat of 'hell fire for sinners' went unheeded.

There could be only one explanation as to why Sare had come here; that he was unable to reach England and had had no alternative.

55

'I have to find him – I must!' Craig thought.

Perturbed by his own thoughts he was so absent-minded at luncheon that his very attractive hostess reproached him for neglecting her, and the lady on his other side said very much the same thing.

Their rebukes immediately reminded Craig that he was not acting the part that was expected of him.

So, excusing himself as having a slight headache, he set out to be his gay, inconsequential and amusing self, which left the two women when the meal ended, more in love with him than they were already.

He had an invitation to play tennis, but he had already had a game with the Professional early in the morning when, on finding it hard to sleep, he had turned to the comforting male solace of hard exercise.

'You must enter for the Lawn Tennis Championships, Sir,' the Pro. said when, after three hard sets, Craig won comparatively easily.

Craig knew that this Championship had been initiated three years previously, and he had in fact thought of entering for the Cup in the Men's Singles which had been presented by the Prince of Monaco.

Then he decided that he had other more interesting and more important things to do than to collect trophies, and preferred to take his exercise without an audience.

Nevertheless he enjoyed playing a game at which he had distinguished himself in America, and he booked the Professional to play with him every morning while he was in Monte Carlo.

However when he was free after luncheon he had no intention of playing anything until he had talked to Father Augustin.

He therefore walked as he had the day before down the hill to the Chapel of *St. Devoté*, entering the quiet incense-filled Church to find there were just a few more worshippers than there had been the day before.

The dimness of the Chapel after the noise and brilliance of the Hotel, which always seemed to be filled with sunshine, made him aware of a peace which came from the faith which it had enshrined for so long and was like a cool hand on his forehead.

56

He stood for a moment to compose his thoughts and, although he was hardly aware of it, to make quite sure there was no-one present in the Church who might recognise him.

Then he walked quietly towards the Confessional and knew as he pushed aside the curtain that Father Augustin was waiting for him.

He knelt down and automatically the Priest said the familiar Latin words which began every confessional.

Then as he said 'Amen' Craig asked:

'Have you any news for me, Father?'

'A little, my son, but you have not given me much time.'

'But you have heard something?'

'I have heard that the man you seek,' Father Augustin replied, and wisely did not mention his name, 'was hiding in a certain place in the town two weeks ago.'

'He is not ill or wounded?'

'There was no reference to that,' the Priest replied, 'but it was understood he was in hiding. The place where he was staying is only used by those who are avoiding the Police, or have other reasons for not wishing to be seen.'

'He is there now?' Craig asked eagerly.

Then he knew as he asked the question that the reply would be disappointing.

'From what I have been able to ascertain,' the Priest replied, 'he has gone.'

'Have you found out where?'

'That is what I am trying to do,' Father Augustin said, 'but you will understand that it is not easy to make enquiries in that particular place where men deliberately hide, and whose identity is always secret.'

'I understand,' Craig said, 'but, please, Father, because it is of the utmost importance, find out more.'

'I am trying, my son, I assure you, I am trying,' Father Augustin replied, 'but it is not easy. If I appear too eager it will inevitably mean that doors will be closed which might otherwise remain open.'

Craig knew that was only too true, and all he could say was:

'I am deeply grateful, Father. This man is of great importance

57

to humanity and somehow with your help I have to save him.'

'I can only rely on God,' Father Augustin replied, 'and I have prayed for His help.'

'Then please continue to do so.'

There was a little pause. Then he added:

'I have something which may help to loosen the tongues of those who know the answers to our questions. Where shall I leave it?'

There was silence for a moment, then Father Augustin replied:

'There is a wreath in front of the effigy of St. Dévoté.'

There was no need for him to say more and Craig asked:

'When shall I come again?'

'Tomorrow I shall be hearing confessions a little later, so I shall be here just when it is growing dark.'

'That will be helpful,' Craig said.

He waited until Father Augustin said the blessing in Latin and when he rose from his knees he pulled aside the curtain of the Confessional.

As he did so he saw there were more people in the Church than there had been when he came in, and when he glanced at them he saw with a sudden leap of excitement that kneeling only a little way from him was the Countess Aloya.

Her clasped hands were resting on the top of the *prie-dieu* at which she was praying, and her head was thrown back a little, her eyes raised to the lamp burning in front of the sanctuary.

She was obviously completely unaware of him, at least that was what she appeared to be, and yet because he was so conscious of her, Craig thought it would be a mistake to walk past her and out of the Church.

Instead he stepped across the narrow aisle and sat down in a seat next to hers.

He did not kneel, but bent forward and put his hand over his eyes as if he was praying.

He was wondering what he should say to her when without moving she said in a voice so low he could only just hear her:

'Please . . do not . . speak to . . me! There is . . somebody . . watching.'

58

Another man might have stared at her in astonishment, or even expostulated, but Craig had been trained in a school where one unwary movement, one slip of the tongue, could mean, if not certain death, discovery.

For the moment he did not move, then as if his prayer was over he rose from his seat and without even looking at the Countess, genuflected in the aisle, then walked deliberately slowly to where the effigy in wax of St. Devoté, to whom the Chapel was dedicated, lay against the North wall.

St. Devoté, the Patron Saint of Monaco, was born in Corsica in AD 283. Her parents were pagan but her Christian name brought her the new faith.

In the great persecution she was tortured which she endured, praying and smiling. As she died her soul flew up to Heaven in the form of a dove.

The same dove piloted the barque which carried her body to Monaco where it settled on a rock and there the Chapel dedicated to her was ultimately built.

Few people who came to Monte Carlo to worship the green tables in the Casino knew of the Chapel but, as he did in everything with which he had any contact, Craig learnt the history and stored what he learnt away in his mind.

He stood for a moment looking at the wax figure of a very young girl with the dove resting on her head.

Then he saw as he expected there was a wreath laid in front of it, obviously commemorating the death of somebody who believed the Saint would pray in Heaven for those who had died on earth.

The green vine leaves, the faded pink and white carnations and the ribbon which tied the wreath at its base were all too familiar even to be noticed.

As Craig knelt as if in reverence in front of the Patron Saint of the Chapel, he slipped an envelope beneath the wreath so quickly that it was doubtful if anybody watching him would have been aware of his action.

Then he rose to his feet and deliberately moved very slowly down the Church.

As he had expected, while he was engaged in looking at the

statue of St. Devoté and leaving a considerable amount of francs for Father Augustin, the Countess had left.

He was sure it had been a move on her part so that those of whom she had spoken as watching would not have seen him, or if they had done so, would have been aware only of his back.

It was something he would have thought of himself, but he was surprised that the Countess had been so astute.

Again at the door of the Church he lingered, picking up some books of prayer, flicking over the pages and pretending to read a leaflet which gave the times of the Services.

Only when he was quite certain that the Countess had driven away, if she had come by carriage, or was out of sight if she had walked, did he leave the Chapel.

He now had a great deal to think about.

It was obvious last night when she had left him so hastily that she must have heard the Russian servant come into the room behind her.

He imagined now that either the maid, which would have been usual, had accompanied her to the Church, or perhaps she had another bodyguard of some sort.

It was so intriguing that Craig found it impossible to think of anything else for the rest of the afternoon.

It was only when he had puzzled over what had been said and found himself wondering how soon he could see the Countess again, that he remembered that the Grand Duke Boris was giving a party that evening, and had been determined to invite her with Lord Neasdon.

As by this time it was after four o'clock Craig was certain the Grand Duke would be in the Casino.

The place was filling up as it inevitably did before dinner and he walked quickly into the *Salle Touzet* and was relieved to see, as he expected, the Grand Duke sitting at the Baccarat table, playing with what to any other man would have been a fortune.

As Craig watched, speaking to one or two of the spectators whom he knew, the Grand Duke lost the pile of notes and gold in front of him and rose to his feet without any expression of annoyance or disappointment on his handsome face.

60

Then as he moved away from the table he saw Craig and put out his hand.

'Come and have a drink with me, Craig,' he said. 'I need it.'

Craig was too wise to commiserate with him over his losses, knowing it was something a gambler hated more than anything else, just as they thought it unlucky to be congratulated on their wins.

'It is rather early for me to drink,' he replied, 'I am keeping myself for your party tonight, if it is still taking place.'

'Of course it is taking place.' the Grand Duke said, 'and Zsi-Zsi has asked all your special friends to meet you, although I expect most of them know already that you are here amongst us.'

'You make me sound as if like Lucifer I dropped from the sky,' Craig smiled.

'A good simile,' the Grand Duke joked. 'I think the mere fact that you are so rich, Craig, brings out the devil in those who know you, and especially in the women who love you.'

'I disagree,' Craig replied, 'but never mind, and thank you in anticipation of tonight. Have you persuaded Neasdon to accept your invitation?'

He thought it would be a mistake to sound too eager. At the same time he had to know.

The Grand Duke laughed.

'He jumped at it like a hungry salmon. I have never invited him before, and I am damned if I would do so now, unless I had a good reason for it.'

'Is he actually bringing the Countess?'

'He said so, but the strange thing is he sounded so sure that he would do so that I had the feeling her opinion would not be asked.'

'Obviously,' Craig said with a cynical note in his voice, 'Neasdon has some hidden charms of which we are not aware.'

'If he has, all I can say is that I am a bad judge of men and women,' the Grand Duke replied, 'something I never imagined I would be. Anyway, tonight you shall see her for yourself and how she clings to Neasdon. Believe it or not, I have never seen her talking to anybody else since she has been here, and it

61

seems to me extraordinary.'

Craig agreed with him, but because he thought it would be a mistake to talk too much about the Countess he changed the conversation to other subjects, then making the excuse that he had an appointment, he went back to the Hotel.

In his own Suite he resisted an impulse to go out onto the balcony which adjoined that of the Countess.

Firstly he knew he had no wish for any of his staff to be aware that he had even entered the empty bedroom, and secondly, he suspected that if the Countess was in her Suite her Russian maid might be with her.

But why she should be frightened of her maid, and why it had been so important that he should not speak to her in the Chapel or appear to know her was a mystery.

They were questions to which he could find no answer and when he was dressing for dinner he had the feeling that he was on the verge of an exciting adventure, and one that seemed so unpredictable that he had no idea of what the outcome might be.

Because it was a feeling he had not had for some time, but which he had known in the past and therefore recognised, Craig felt as if there was a new pulsation of power flowing through him.

It was something he had always felt when he was in danger or when he was engaged on some of the strange missions with which he had been entrusted by the Marquess.

Because it was so utterly different from his life both in New York and in London as a rich, carefree young man, he cherished and enjoyed the challenge which these missions gave him.

He knew now that if he was to be successful he would need all the mysterious, mystic power which he had always called on in an emergency.

He had not forgotten that he wished to know more about the Russian yachts, and on returning from the Casino, before he went upstairs to his Suite he had gone to the Manager's office.

The Manager of the *Hôtel de Paris* was one of the best informed men in the whole of the Principality.

It was his business not only to be aware of the background of every person who stayed in the Hotel, but because it was so closely allied with the Casino the habitues of the green tables also came under his surveillance.

If there was one thing the authorities detested it was a scandal or a suicide and every possible precaution was taken to see that anything that could reflect badly upon the reputation of Monte Carlo as a whole must be prevented from taking place.

If unfortunately that was impossible, then what occurred must be swept out of sight as quickly and as discreetly as possible.

Monsieur Bleuet was therefore a man of discretion besides having a sharp and intelligent brain which missed very little.

Because it was almost certain that to *Monsieur* Bleuet Craig was exactly what he appeared, a wealthy American in search of amusement, Craig knew he must phrase what he had to say as carefully as possible.

'I hope, *Monsieur* Vandervelt,' the Manager said, 'that you are comfortable. Is there anything I can do for you?'

'I came to tell you that I am very comfortable,' Craig answered, 'and it was exceedingly kind of you to let me have the same Suite that I had last year, and the year before that.'

Monsieur Bleuet smiled.

'We try always, *Monsieur*, to make our favourite clients feel at home, and to do that it is important they occupy the same rooms they have used before and have if possible the same room service.'

'I appreciate that,' Craig said, 'but I also want to ask you what you know about the two Russian yachts in the harbour.'

He smiled as he said:

'It may sound just curiosity, but as it happens I am anxious, if they are new, to compare them with my own yacht, which I like to think is more advanced than any other vessel afloat.'

'I have always heard, *Monsieur* Vandervelt, that *'The Mermaid'* is the envy of every yachtsman in the harbour, and quite exceptional as regards its engine, its steering and the new gadgets you have yourself installed.'

Craig smiled complacently and knew that what *Monsieur*

63

Bleuet was saying was what he might have expected him to know.

'I went over the Duke of Westminster's yacht last year,' he replied, 'and I know it does not compare with *'The Mermaid'*. The same applies to Mr. Pierpont Morgan's boat which is old, and it is time he bought a new one.'

Monsieur Bleuet laughed.

'It is something he can certainly afford.'

'I suppose when one gets older, one becomes attached to one's possessions,' Craig remarked. 'I can understand that, as I am sure you can, when it concerns something like a picture, but for me where yachts and motor cars are concerned, the newer the better.'

Monsieur Bleuet laughed again.

'I might almost say the same, *Monsieur*, in the case of *Les Femmes*!'

'Now that is a different subject altogether,' Craig said, 'but we were speaking of the Russian yachts.'

'Yes, of course,' the Manager agreed. 'But I regret to say that I have never been aboard either of them, and in fact I do not know anybody who has.'

'Do you mean to say that their owners do not entertain?'

'Their *owner, Monsieur*.'

'Only one?'

'Yes, Baron Strogoloff is his name, and he is an invalid.'

'Oh, that explains everything!'

'Not exactly,' the Manager said. 'The Baron has some affliction of the legs, I understand, which necessitates his being always in a wheel-chair. He is pushed around the deck of his yacht, and he also comes to the Casino.'

'To gamble?'

The Manager shook his head.

'No. They tell me he is fond of music, so he attends the Concerts and the Operas that take place in the Theatre.'

'He does not gamble?'

'*Monsieur Le Baron* has not yet entered the *Salle Touzet*, which you will understand is very sad for us since he is, I believe, amazingly rich.'

'And when he leaves, he will take it all with him!'

Craig laughed before he added:

'That of course is a tragedy, but he must be very eccentric to need two yachts.'

'*Monsieur Le Baron* uses one himself, and the other is for his guests and those who wait on him.'

'That is certainly luxury,' Craig remarked. 'And what are his guests like?'

'You will hardly credit this, *Monsieur*,' the Manager replied, 'but in Monte Carlo, of all places, they stay on board and never come ashore.'

'I do not believe it,' Craig exclaimed. 'It seems incredible!'

'That is what we all feel,' the Manager said, 'and our discussions about the Baron have taken up a great deal of time when we meet officially.'

'I am quite sure about that,' Craig smiled. 'And what does the Prince Albert think about it?'

'We have not yet had the privilege of discussing it with His Royal Highness,' the Manager answered, 'but now you mention it, perhaps he, and he alone, could persuade the Baron to be a little more sociable.'

'I doubt it,' Craig said. 'These Russians are always unpredictable, and you can thank goodness you have people like the charming and very extravagant Grand Dukes.

'There I agree with you, *Monsieur* Vandervelt, we are very, very lucky. As the Grand Duke Michael was saying to me only yesterday, when he goes back to Russia he counts the days until he can return to us, and what he refers to as his "home from home".'

The complacency in the Manager's voice told Craig how much the Russian Grand Duke contributed to the huge profits the Casino was making every year.

Because such details interested him, he was well aware that the shareholders were becoming millionaires, and the other resorts were grinding their teeth in fury at the success achieved by Monaco.

They talked for a little longer, but Craig deliberately did not mention the Countess.

Then because he knew it would please the Manager and even increase his own prestige, he spoke of his delight in finding so many distinguished visitors in Monte Carlo, including Prince Radziwell, who had brought his own polo ponies, the Duke of Montrose and the beautiful Duchess of Marlborough, who was an American.

The Manager had something interesting to say about each one of them, but Craig, having learnt what he had come to find out, was not listening.

When he reached his own Suite he stood for a long time at the window looking at the two Russian yachts side by side in the harbour below.

. . . .

The Grand Duke's Villa was a dream of Oriental magnificence; a mixture of Russian taste which ran to copulas and domes and an endless profusion of gold.

It also combined every possible Western comfort which involved huge over-padded sofas and armchairs, velvet hangings, and pictures which any connoisseur of art would have given his right arm to possess.

Each Oriental rug on the floor was a poem in needlework and the gold ornaments which decorated the dinner-table were priceless not only in their antiquity, but because they were ornamented with the most magnificent precious stones the Siberian mines could produce.

There were orchids everywhere, and yet because his guests were so glamorous they were not overshadowed by their surroundings.

As usual before one of his parties the Grand Duke gave a dinner party for about fifty of his personal friends, and then acquaintances arrived afterwards from midnight until dawn.

Looking down the long table with the gold plate off which they were to eat, with crystal glasses which shone like diamonds and were emblazoned with the Grand Duke's insignia, Craig was aware that neither the Countess nor Neasdon was there.

It was what he had expected, but nevertheless he was disappointed. He had wanted to look at her, perhaps to re-affirm that she was as beautiful as she had appeared the night before.

It seemed incredible that he had not seen her during the day, except for when she had been praying in the Church, and he wondered where she hid herself when she was not with Neasdon.

It was then as he looked more closely at the other guests that he realised the Grand Duke had finally made up his mind into which category she belonged.

The other men were all of great importance, aristocrats to their finger-tips and, Craig thought a little cynically, with the exception of himself entirely European or Russian, the women extremely beautifully dressed but undoubtedly belonging to the *demi-monde*.

This was not to say that they were not delightful companions in public as well as in private.

Because of their profession they had manners as beautiful as their faces, and it was an unwritten law that they never embarrassed their protector by trying to meet his family.

Craig knew from past experience that their behaviour at the gaming tables was exemplary, and they never created scenes as Society Ladies were sometimes prone to do.

The Cocottes wore, as might have been expected, the most superb jewellery. Their gowns which came from the most famous Houses in Paris, the majority designed by Frederick Worth, would have graced any Royal Palace.

But even in Monte Carlo where everything from a social point of view was far more lax than anywhere else, *les femmes de joie* never attempted to cross the dividing line between the *Monde* and the *demi-Monde*.

The only additions to the famous Cocottes like La Belle Otero and Gaby Delys at the party were a few women of blue blood who had thrown away for love, their position in Society.

Craig recognised a Marchioness who had run away from a drunken and brutal husband to live in what the world called 'sin' with a French *Duc*, who already had a wife and a large number of children whom he left in a Château in the country and seldom saw.

There was also the daughter of a very well-known British Earl who had been twice divorced and was still lovely and attractive enough to be considering taking a third husband, who was sitting beside her gazing adoringly into her eyes and obviously completely uninterested in anybody else in the room.

It all seemed somewhat familiar, a scene Craig had witnessed a dozen times before, but which he enjoyed aesthetically and would have enjoyed even more if a new face in the shape of the Countess Aloya Zladamir had been there.

Then he told himself he must wait in patience until dinner was over and the Grand Duke's other guests arrived, and he forced himself to be pleasant to his dinner companions.

This was not a very difficult task, as they had been trained in a hard school to amuse any man they were with and make him find them desirable.

As was usual in France, the ladies and gentlemen all left the Dining Room together.

When they walked into the large Salon where they had been before dinner and which opened onto another one equally spacious where the furniture had been cleared away so that they could dance, Craig saw the Countess.

She was standing at an open window looking out onto the garden which was lit with a thousand small candles fluttering in the evening breeze, and huge Chinese lanterns glowing golden in the branches of the trees.

There was the scent of mimosa which was in flower, and Craig seeing the Countess's profile against the sky thought it would be impossible for any woman to look so lovely.

In fact she seemed part of the night itself.

He had wondered, after her dramatic appearance last night, if she could equal the sensation her black gown had caused in the Dining Room of the *Hôtel de Paris*.

He thought that now she was in fact even more spectacular in a gown that was of silver like the moonlight outside and seemed to cling to her slim figure, except where the skirt billowed out around her feet.

Because it shone from the moonlight on one side of the

Countess and in the light from the chandeliers on the other, she seemed almost to be enveloped in running water, a nymph from the sea without human substance.

He did not approach her, but just stood looking at her. He saw as she turned her face towards the Grand Duke as he advanced across the room to greet her, that her only jewel tonight was a huge diamond star which she wore on top of her head and which seemed to melt into the shining silver of her hair.

As she curtsied to the Grand Duke, he thought it would be impossible for a woman to be more graceful.

Then the Grand Duke, extremely affably, was welcoming Lord Neasdon and there was no doubt that the Englishman was extremely gratified.

There was a band of twenty violins already playing in the next salon, and to Craig's mind it seemed to make the whole scene dreamlike and without reality.

There was also, he knew, another room in which there were the inevitable green tables where the Grand Duke's guests could lose their money at every known game of chance without having to go to the Casino.

As he might have expected, the female guests were already eagerly luring their partners to the table where the Roulette wheel was spinning, or to another where *trente et quarante* was a quick way to win or lose.

It was accepted that a gentleman gave half his winnings to the lady who accompanied him besides giving her enough to play herself, should she wish to do so.

The Grand Duke had moved away from Lord Neasdon to greet other guests who were now arriving in large numbers and the Countess was once again looking out of the window while Lord Neasdon talked to her.

Craig decided that if he was going to make her acquaintance formally he would have to take the matter into his own hands.

This was made easy by the fact that he saw that Zsi-Zsi, who was acting as hostess during the evening, was for the moment standing alone.

Although she was known to be living with the Grand Duke

69

and was always with him when he was in Monte Carlo while his wife remained in Russia, Zsi-Zsi, because she had been married to a respectable French Comte, was accepted by quite a number of social hostesses.

It would therefore have been possible if the Grand Duke had wished to invite only the 'crème de la crème' to his party for Zsi-Zsi still to be there.

Craig did not question that the Grand Duke had finally decided the status of the Countess and Zsi-Zsi had arranged the party accordingly.

He walked over to her, took her arm and said to her quietly:

'You have made me curious about the newcomer, so the least you can do is introduce me to her.'

'I think it would be a mistake, Craig,' Zsi-Zsi replied. 'She is quite obviously tied up with Lord Neasdon, and there are several women here tonight who have begged me to ensure they have an opportunity to be with you, including the one who was on your right at dinner.'

'I still wish to meet the Countess.'

Zsi-Zsi shrugged her shoulders.

'Very well, if you insist, but do not blame me if you get a "set down" such as poor Boris received, althought he tried to keep it a secret from me!'

Craig's eyes twinkled remembering what the Grand Duke had said to him, but he merely said:

'I will risk it, and if my morale is damaged, I can always come to you for consolation.'

'Which you are quite certain I will give you,' Zsi-Zsi said mockingly.

As they were talking Craig had deliberately moved her across the Salon to where the Countess and Lord Neasdon were standing.

Now, as they reached them the Countess turned her head from her contemplation of the garden and looked at Zsi-Zsi in a way that Craig thought was almost as if she was shy.

Then he told himself it was ridiculous to think such a thing, and it must just be a clever trick which would undoubtedly endear her to an older woman and certainly to any man.

'How nice to see you, Countess,' Zsi-Zsi gushed, 'and Lord Neasdon, His Imperial Highness is so delighted you could come this evening. He had been wanting to make your acquaintance for a long time.'

'You are very kind, *Madame*,' Lord Neasdon replied.

'And now as you are our guest for the first time,' Zsi-Zsi said, 'I insist that you open the Ball with me. The band is playing *"The Blue Danube"*, and what could be a more delightful dance with which to start our acquaintance?'

As Zsi-Zsi smiled up into Lord Neasdon's face it would have been impossible for any man to refuse her such a request, but diplomatically Lord Neasdon hesitated and glanced at the Countess.

'*Tiens*! I forgot!' Zsi-Zsi exclaimed in her bird-like voice. '*Madame la Comtesse*, allow me to introduce to you Mr. Craig Vandervelt, who will look after you while I dance with the charming Lord Neasdon.'

She paused to add impressively:

'Mr. Vandervelt is American, but as he is so very rich we forgive him for choosing to live in such a far off part of the world.'

She laughed as she spoke, and it was like the joyous twittering of a songbird.

Then without saying any more she drew Lord Neasdon by the hand into the next room.

Craig moved two paces nearer to the Countess and stood looking at her.

She did not speak and turned her face towards the garden.

'I have been waiting for this moment!' he said in his deep voice, 'and because we have a lot to say to each other and I have no wish to be disturbed, shall we go outside?'

CHAPTER FOUR

For a moment Craig thought the Countess was going to refuse. Then she looked over her shoulder nervously and he knew she was wondering if Lord Neasdon was watching her.

However he had already vanished into the adjoining Salon and, as if the Countess felt released from some restraint which Craig could not understand, she walked quickly through the open French window into the garden.

There were not many people moving across the lawn, and under the trees Craig deliberately put his hand under the Countess's elbow and guided her to where there were fewer lights.

Having been in the Grand Duke's garden several times before, he knew there were seats made comfortable with silk cushions, and there were also small arbours which covered with climbing vines, were places where those who wished could be private and unobserved.

They walked without speaking. Then as he turned towards one of the arbours which was only faintly lit by lanterns hanging from an adjacent tree he feared at first that the Countess would protest.

But as if he read her thoughts he knew she was aware, as he was, that in the arbour they would not be seen, and she allowed him to pilot her there.

As Craig expected, the seat inside was covered with soft cushions and as they sat down he looked back the way they had come and saw that they were alone in this part of the garden where there were no fairy-lights.

He turned to sit sideways on the seat with his arm along the back of it and said:

'Now at last I can talk to you as I am very anxious to do.'

He spoke in a voice which most women found irresistibly beguiling, but the Countess did not look at him and only stared ahead. He could just see the outline of her straight little nose.

'What do you . . want to talk . . about?' she asked, and there was a quiver in her voice.

'About you,' Craig replied, 'but it is difficult to know where to begin.'

'I do not . . think we have . . anything to say to . . each other.'

'I have a great deal to say,' he argued, 'but first I want to know why you are frightened, and of whom?'

He knew that she stiffened, then she said quickly:

'Please . . I think we should . . go back. I am sure . . Lord Neasdon will want to . . dance with . . me.'

'He has only just begun to dance with our hostess,' Craig replied, 'and as she is undoubtedly with the exception of yourself, the most alluring woman here, I do not think he will be in any hurry to change partners.'

If he thought he was being reassuring he was mistaken; for the Countess appeared to be even more tense than before, and he saw that her fingers in her long white gloves were clasped together, twining and inter-twining with each other.

Craig bent a little nearer. Then he said very quietly:

'Let me help you. If you are in trouble, I will get you out of it, and I promise I will free you from being afraid as you are now.'

'No one . . can do . . that.'

He could hardly hear the words, and yet they were spoken. 'Why not?'

She did not answer and after a moment he said:

'I am aware there is something wrong, very, very wrong. You are the most beautiful woman in the whole of Monte Carlo. Everybody is anxious to meet you, every man is at your feet, and yet you are being menaced by some fear, and that is

73

something I must bring to an end.'

As his voice died away the Countess clenching and unclenching her hands said pleadingly:

'Please . . do not talk to me like this . . I want help . . desperately . . but I cannot ask . . you for it . . nor anybody else.'

'And yet I believe I am the only person who can help you.'

She turned her face further away from him, and he went on:

'You and I have both been in India. We know that strange things can happen there about which the Western world knows little, that thought is used to enable two people to have an inner knowledge of each other, however many miles they are apart.'

She did not speak, but he knew a little quiver passed through her, and he said:

'I know you need me, and I know that I am the one person who would be able to help you. I think you know it too.'

Now she looked at him and replied almost passionately:

'How can . . you talk to me . . like this? How are you . . able to . . understand?'

'You know the answer to that,' Craig said. 'There is no need for us to waste time in proving it to each other.'

'But . . how can I be . . sure? You are a man I have . . never seen . . before.'

'And yet you warned me that it was dangerous to speak to you this afternoon in Church,' Craig said. 'Why should you do that if you did not already think of me as being far from a total stranger?'

'I . . I do not know . . anything,' the Countess replied. 'I am so . . frightened . . terribly frightened . . and yet I dare not . . trust you.'

There was a frantic note in her voice and Craig deliberately waited a moment before he replied very quietly:

'Do not listen to your brain, listen to our instinct, as you would if you were in India and the same Guru was teaching us.'

She drew in her breath. Then just as he thought she was about to confide in him she said in a whisper:

74

'Suppose . . somebody is . . listening?'

'Here?' Craig enquired. 'I think it is very unlikely, but if there is somebody watching you, tell me why.'

'I . . I cannot do . . that,' the Countess said with a little sob, 'but they are watching . . they are always watching . . and although I cannot always . . see them . . I know they are there.'

'Who are they? And why?'

Even as he asked the questions he knew perceptively that she was not going to answer him, and that her fear was rising in her, seeping through her body and into her mind, so that it was impossible for her to think clearly.

'Now listen to me,' he said in a low voice. 'I understand your difficulties better than you think I do. What I want you to remember is that I am here, and I can and will help you as nobody else in the world can do.'

She did not speak but looked away again, and he went on:

'Your room connects with mine and what I am going to do when I get back to the Hotel is to unlock the communicating door on my side. If you want me at any moment, slide a piece of paper under the door from your side and I will open the door between us without anyone being aware of it.'

He knew she was listening attentively to what he was saying and he went on:

'Or if you wish, we can talk on the balcony, but only when you feel it is safe.'

She looked at him fleetingly for a moment. Then she said in a whisper:

'Thank you . . I shall remember . . but please . . do not come to the Church again in the afternoon . . they might . . realise that our rooms are . . near to each other.'

'I understand,' Craig answered, 'but if you will tell me who "they" are, it might be easier for me to help you.'

As if his question agitated her almost unbearably she said quickly:

'No . . no . . I cannot stay . . I dare not . . please . . forget we have . . talked together like this.'

'I think the truth is it is I who talked,' Craig smiled. 'But at

75

least you know I am here, and if you are afraid then I am prepared to tackle anyone or anything to wipe the tears from your eyes.'

Even in the dim light he could see a little smile that was somehow pathetic. Then she rose to her feet.

'I must go back . . I am sure the dance is . . over.'

'Walk slowly and casually,' Craig said. 'If, as you fear, someone is watching, they will think if you hurry that you have something to hide.'

He saw her eyes widen, then as she stepped from the arbour she said in a voice that was different from what she had been using:

'How delightful it must be to have a garden like this and to know that almost all the year round it is full of flowers!'

Craig knew she was speaking as if somebody might overhear her and he replied lightly:

'In my opinion the *Côte d'Azur* is never lovelier than when the minosa trees are golden and the first hibiscus comes into bloom.'

He deliberately moved slowly and knew the Countess took her pace from him.

Only as they got back to the lights thrown from the windows of the Villa did he see that she was very pale, and at the same time in her glittering silver gown and with the star on her silver hair she looked ethereal and hardly human.

Now they were moving amongst the other people returning from the garden into the house and as they walked in through a French window Craig saw Lord Neasdon and Zsi-Zsi coming from the other Salon where they had been dancing.

He sensed that at the sight of Lord Neasdon the Countess seemed to shudder, and he had the feeling, although he was not sure why, that she recoiled from him and moved as if instinctively closer to himself.

'We have had the most delightful dance,' Zsi-Zsi said in her attractive voice. 'His Lordship is a very good dancer.'

'Surely that is unusual for an Englishman?' Craig remarked. 'I hope you will introduce me, as we have not yet met.'

'*Oo La! La!* How remiss of me!' Zsi-Zsi exclaimed. 'Lord Neasdon, this is Craig Vandervelt, a very charming American who honours us with his presence here in Monte Carlo nearly every year, and we women look forward to his arrival with pulpitating hearts.'

Lord Neasdon held out his hand.

'How do you do!' he said rather heavily. 'I have heard of you, although we have never met.'

'I think you work in the Foreign Office with a relative of mine, the Marquess of Lansdowne.'

'He is a relative of yours?' Lord Neasdon asked in surprise.

'A distant cousin.'

'I had no idea!'

'I see him from time to time,' Craig answered, 'but I live in America when I am at home, which is not very often.'

Zsi-Zsi laughed.

'I can tell you that Craig is an inveterate traveller who goes round and round the world like a meteor, if that is the right description.'

'You must find it very interesting,' Lord Neasdon said.

It was obvious as he spoke that he was not at all interested in the conversation, and his eyes were on the Countess. Craig was aware that she was looking at him with an expression he could not understand.

It seemed almost as if she was pleading with him, and at the same time he had the feeling that she was trying to attract him but did not really know how to do so.

There followed an uncomfortable silence when nobody could think of anything else to say, until Craig bowed to the Countess.

'I hope I may have the pleasure of dancing with you later this evening,' he said. 'May I say it has been delightful meeting you.'

Then without waiting for a reply he moved to Zsi-Zsi's side saying:

'Let me congratulate an old friend whose party is, as usual, perfection, and why should I expect it to be anything else?'

'That is very nicely said, *Mon Cher*,' Zsi-Zsi replied

77

slipping her arm through his and drawing him away leaving Lord Neasdon and the Countess alone.

When they were out of ear-shot, Zsi-Zsi said:

'*Oo la, la*! I hope you are grateful. Never have I met a more boring man who can talk only of himself.'

'I *am* grateful.'

'That lovely woman! What can she see in him?' Zsi-Zsi asked. 'He has nothing interesting to say, he dances like an elephant, and is so conceited that he believed me when I said he was a good dancer.'

'Suppose you dance with me?' Craig said. 'Then you can forget Neasdon.'

'I would love it later,' Zsi-Zsi replied, 'but first I must see if there is anything Boris wants, and greet some new arrivals.'

She moved away, and as she did so Craig was aware that Lord Neasdon was taking the Countess into the garden.

It suddenly struck him that if she had been afraid their conversation would be overheard, there was no reason why he should not listen to theirs.

The Band was playing a spirited dance which had brought almost all the guests except those sitting at the card-tables onto the dance-floor.

Casually, as if he was enjoying the night air, Craig walked out under the trees and saw Lord Neasdon and the Countess moving down the path lit with fairy-lights to the arbours on the other side of the garden from where he had taken her.

He watched them until he saw with satisfaction that they moved into an arbour which was surrounded by bushes and lit by several Chinese lanterns in the overhanging trees.

Only as they disappeared out of view did he move swiftly in the direction of the shrubs, and walking quietly through them he went to the back of the arbour in which they were now sitting.

As he reached it he heard Lord Neasdon's voice say:

'You are enjoying yourself?'

'Very much,' the Countess replied. 'It is very kind of you to bring me to such a . . delightful party.'

'The Grand Duke Boris gives them very frequently when

78

he is in Monte Carlo.'

'He is very distinguished.'

'I believe a number of women find him so,' Lord Neasdon said somewhat contemptuously.

'It is . . strange,' the Countess said a little tentatively, 'that there should be so many English people at the party when I thought the English were angry with the Russians.'

'Why should you think that?'

'I heard . . although it may be wrong . . that there is . . friction between the Russians and the English . . concerning India.'

There was silence, almost as if Lord Neasdon was thinking what he should say. Then he replied:

'You must not believe all you hear.'

'But it is true, is it not, that the Russians have made the British Government . . very angry?'

'I do not know what you have heard,' Lord Neasdon said, 'but there is always a lot of tittle-tattle if there is any movement of troops, and if a few shots are fired on the Frontier it becomes a "battle".'

There was a little silence. Then the Countess said:

'You do not . . think there could be . . war between our . . two nations? That would be . . terrible!'

'There is no fear of that,' Lord Neasdon said, 'and I assure you the British have the whole situation very well in hand.'

'You mean they will not . . allow there to be a war, even if Russia should . . wish it?'

Lord Neasdon laughed unpleasantly.

'The English can stand up to the Russians, and if there are a few scuffles between us on the North-West frontier, they would not defeat us.'

'You are quite . . sure of . . that?'

'Very, very sure.'

The Countess gave a little sigh.

'That means that the British have lots of troops in India to prevent any Russian . . infiltration into . . Afghanistan.'

She spoke as if she was afraid of the idea, and Lord Neasdon said:

79

'Now do not worry your pretty head, Aloya. I promise you there will be no war, and even if there is one I will look after you and protect you.'

'That might be .. difficult if our .. countries are .. enemies.'

'I shall never be your enemy,' he said. 'Let me show you how well I will look after you.'

He must have put his arm around the Countess for Craig listening heard her give a little scream as she said:

'No .. no .. please, you must not do that .. here! It would be very .. indiscreet.'

'Nobody can see us,' Lord Neasdon objected, 'and you know quite well you are driving me mad! You promised you would let me love you when we knew each other better, and I think it is time you began to keep your promise.'

'We .. have known .. each other such a .. little time,' the Countess said in a voice that sounded terrified.

'Long enough for me to know that I want you and love you!' Lord Neasdon said. 'Why should you be faithful to this husband of yours who allows you to wander about the world alone instead of looking after you as he should do?'

'He is still .. my husband and I am .. fond of him.'

'If he was fond of you he would look after you properly,' Lord Neasdon said firmly. 'But I am here, and you have told me you find me interesting and attractive, while I find you adorable and very, very desirable.'

He paused, and when she did not speak he added:

'Let me come to your room tonight and show you how much you mean to me, and how happy we could be together.'

'Oh .. no .. not tonight,' the Countess said hastily. 'It is .. too soon, much .. too soon.'

There was a frantic, desperate note in her voice as she said:

'You know I like to be with you, I like to talk to you and listen to you. You are so interesting and you can teach me so much about the world .. a world of which I know very .. little.'

'A world in which you shine brilliantly!' Lord Neasdon said. 'There is no woman in the whole of Monte Carlo to equal you, and I am very proud.'

He spoke in a complacent manner which made Craig feel that he wanted to hit him as he went on:

'Now that the Grand Duke has asked us here tonight we shall have many invitations together, and I think I can introduce you to people you would otherwise not meet, and whom you will find very interesting.'

'I am quite . . content to be with . . you,' the Countess said in a small voice. 'You talk to me of . . all the things I . . want to know.'

'I want to talk about ourselves,' Lord Neasdon said, 'and quite frankly, Aloya, it does not particularly concern me whether our countrymen prance about on the North-West Frontier or try to invade Tibet when all I want is to invade your bedroom.'

There was a little silence. Then the Countess said:

'That might be just . . as difficult as . . invading Tibet!'

'I am a very determined man.'

'I keep . . thinking of . . my husband.'

'Then forget him!'

'I try . . but it is . . difficult.'

'Not for me.'

The Countess gave a little laugh which Craig was certain was forced.

'Am I . . really like . . Tibet?'

'Of course you are,' Lord Neasdon said, 'mysterious, unknown, and impenetrable, except of course, to me!'

'That is very complimentary, but perhaps the . . barriers which will keep out the Russians will also prove . . impenetrable to you.'

'That is for you to say, but I am confident that whatever barriers and obstacles there are, I shall be able to sweep them away. Let me kiss you now, and show you how easily they can vanish when one is in love.'

'No . . no . . this is not the . . right place! I would be very . . embarrassed to go back into the Salon looking . . dishevelled.'

Lord Neasdon did not reply, and somehow Craig was aware that the Countess had risen to her feet.

'We shall be .. talked about,' she said, 'if we stay here for too long, and that would be .. bad for your reputation as .. well as .. mine. After all .. you are a very important and .. distinguished member of the .. British Foreign Office.'

'I am glad you think so,' Lord Neasdon replied, 'and perhaps you are right. We can talk about ourselves later when we return to the Hotel.'

'That would be a .. mistake!' the Countess said quickly. 'If you came into my room my maid .. might talk and my husband is very .. jealous.'

'Damn and blast him!' Lord Neasdon said with more feeling in his voice than there had been before.

Craig was aware that they were now out of the arbour and moving back towards the Villa, their voices gradually fading into the distance until he could hear them no more.

He stood where he was behind the arbour thinking it would be a mistake to move until they were completely out of sight.

He knew now that the Marquess had been right in thinking that the Countess was a Russian spy, who was attempting to obtain information from Lord Neasdon.

It had been a mistake on his part to mention Tibet. At the same time Craig was aware that the Countess's efforts were extremely amateurish and very obvious to any man who was not puffed up with his own conceit.

Lord Neasdon must surely be aware of what was happening, and yet Craig had the feeling that he was so naïve, and perhaps in a way so blinded by desire, that he was oblivious of the dangers he was in and of those who were using the Countess as a tool.

As he moved slowly and by a different route back into the garden and then to the Villa, he knew that whatever the Countess was doing she was not doing it willingly.

He was in fact, quite certain that the Russians who were making her act as a spy on their behalf had ordered her to take Lord Neasdon as her lover and she was fighting desperately not to do so.

He had listened closely to every intonation in her voice while she was speaking to Lord Neasdon.

She was not only afraid, as she had confessed to being when she was with him, but twisting and turning with the desperate agility of a small animal to extricate herself from the situation in which she found herself.

When he went over it step by step Craig thought it had been clever of the Russians in the first place to find anybody so spectacular and so unusually beautiful to work in a place where beautiful women of every class abounded.

It was however obvious that this was her first assignment, and Craig was willing to wager a very large sum of money that she had taken it on because she had been forced to do so.

Therefore he had to discover why she was so frightened of her Russian masters that she had to obey them, and secondly how he could help her personally as well as prevent her from obtaining information from Lord Neasdon which the Foreign Office had been afraid he might be indiscreet enough to disclose.

It seemed to Craig absolutely incredible that in his position Lord Neasdon should not realise that it was unthinkable for him to take a Russian mistress at this particular moment when the reports from India were so serious.

And yet he supposed that Neasdon, having had all his experience in the Diplomatic Service in European Capitals, had had little contact with Russians or knowledge of their aspirations in the East.

It was, in fact, known only to a few people at the moment that Russia might be contemplating an invasion of Tibet, which was perturbing men of authority in India and the heads of the Foreign Office in London.

Yet according to the Marquess, Neasdon had learnt enough for it to be important that on that subject, if on nothing else, he must keep his mouth shut.

Craig was quite certain that the fact that he had mentioned Tibet at all, would be immediately repeated by the Countess to whoever was taking her reports back to a higher authority.

It was then that it suddenly struck him that Baron Strogoloff might be playing some part in this strange situation.

It was certainly a mystery that there should be two of his yachts in Monte Carlo, and that his guests, if he had any, never came ashore, and he came only to attend the Theatre.

'One thing is obvious,' Craig said to himself, 'I have somehow to make the acquaintance of the Baron.'

Then as he reached the lighted windows of the Villa he walked in smiling, determined to assume once more the guise of an American Playboy as he went to find Zsi-Zsi and dance with her.

. . . .

The following morning, having played four strenuous sets of Tennis and seen his latest motor car which he was confident would win first prize in the *Concours d'Elégance* Craig strolled onto the terrace below the Casino before luncheon.

Every head was turned in his direction, hands were held out to him in greeting, and he completed almost a Royal progress before he saw seated at a table Lord Neasdon and the Countess.

They were looking rather gloomy and he thought, although he could not be sure, that as he walked up to them there was a sudden light in the Countess's strange and beautiful eyes.

'Good-morning, *Madame*!' he said sweeping his yachting-cap from his head. 'Good-morning, Neasdon! Did you enjoy the party last night?'

'Very much,' Lord Neasdon replied. 'The Grand Duke lived up to his reputation of being an excellent host.'

'I did not stay very late,' Craig said, 'I went on to another party which was actually not so amusing.'

The truth was that he had left immediately after he had danced with Zsi-Zsi and on arrival at the *Hôtel de Paris* had waited in the adjoining room to the Countess's in case she should need him.

Whatever the difficulties, she had obviously persuaded Lord Neasdon to leave her alone that night and the only voice he heard in her room was that of her Russian maid.

Craig had opened the communicating door on his side quite

easily without invoking the aid of a servant.

There were few doors that stayed locked to him after the years in which he had undertaken missions for the Marquess, and silently with hardly a creak the door had surrendered to his expert hands.

Once it was open he could hear quite clearly everything that was said in the next room.

He knew only a smattering of Russian, finding it a very difficult language, but he had learnt enough to know that the maid with what he thought was an impertinent presumption was asking the Countess questions about the evening, and she was answering in monosyllables.

Only when she presumably was undressed and ready for bed had the maid left her, saying good-night and closing the outer door noisily behind her.

It was then that Craig had debated whether he should knock and tell the Countess he was there, but quickly decided it would be a mistake.

Because she was so frightened, so sure she was being watched, the Russians might easily be tricking her into a false sense of security when they were actually still keeping her under observation.

He therefore waited for an hour in case she slipped a piece of paper under the door, but when she did not do so, he put the door on his side very quietly back into place and went to bed.

As he stood at their table there was really nothing Lord Neasdon could do except say:

'Do sit down! Would you like a drink?'

'That is very kind of you,' Craig answered, 'but I must not stay long. I have promised to meet some friends, but they are not here yet.'

As Lord Neasdon called a waiter and asked for a glass of sherry, Craig turned towards the Countess and enquired conversationally:

'Did you enjoy yourself last night?'

'It was a lovely party,' the Countess replied, 'and very, very kind of Lord Neasdon to take me with him.'

85

'You are lucky I know so many people in Monte Carlo,' Lord Neasdon replied, then he said to Craig: 'I have promised the Countess that I shall be able to take her to quite a number of parties because, as you know only too well, Vandervelt, there are half-a-dozen taking place nearly every night.'

'Yes, indeed,' Craig agreed, 'although some of them are doubtless extremely boring.'

'That is what I have found,' Lord Neasdon agreed, 'but one can always pick and choose.'

'Yes, of course.'

The sherry was put down beside him and he took a sip before he said:

'There seem to be a dozen more ships here than there were yesterday. Have you been aboard the Russian yachts?'

Craig asked the question of the Countess without seeming to have any particular reason for doing so.

Then as he saw a sudden shocked expression in her eyes, he knew that he had put his finger unerringly on something he should have been aware of before.

There was a perceptible pause before she answered: 'No, no . . I have not,' but he knew that she lied.

After lunching with his friends and taking one of them on a drive to Mont Agel Craig went to the Chapel of St. Dévoté after it was dark.

He entered the Church tentatively just in case he was too early and the Countess was there. But there was no sign of her, and he walked quickly to the Confessional, sure that in the darkness relieved only by the candles in front of the Saints, he would be unobserved.

Father Augustin was waiting for him and said as soon as he knelt down:

'I have some news for you, my son.'

'I would be greatly relieved to hear it, Father.'

'I am afraid it will not be what you wish to hear.'

'Tell me!'

'The man you seek left his lodgings because he was afraid. I could not find out why, or where he was going, but he had somewhere to go.'

Father Augustin paused for a moment. Then he said:

'My informant thinks he was either misled into a belief that his new hiding-place would be better than the old, or else it was a trap. Anyway, before he could reach his destination two men apprehended him and took him to the harbour.'

Craig stiffened, then knew exactly what he was going to hear.

'He was taken aboard the Russian yacht, *Tsarevitch* which is lying beside the *Tsarina*.'

Craig sighed.

'Thank you, Father. I am more grateful than I can say in words.'

'I am already grateful to you, my son, for your gratitude yesterday.'

'Which I will express even more fully as I leave.'

'Thank you. If I can help you again you have only to come here at this time.'

'You have never failed me, Father, and I need your prayers as I have never needed them before.'

'You know they are yours.'

The Priest blessed him and Craig felt as if the sincerity of it remained with him as he went back to the Hotel.

He was well aware that not only would he need Father Augustin's prayers and the help of God, but the power of every religion with which he had ever associated himself if he was to save Randall Sare from the Russians.

He was quite certain they would stop at nothing to extract from him the information they needed so vitally, and the stories of the tortures they used on prisoners were not only horrifying but, as Craig was aware, not exaggerated.

As he dressed for dinner with the help of his valet he was thinking frantically that it was surprising that having taken him prisoner they had not already left Monte Carlo for Russia.

The only explanation he could think of was that they were expecting to obtain some more information on Tibet from Neasdon.

They would not be aware that what he knew was very little,

87

but even a little added to what Randall Sare could tell them would give them a great advantage in their position which up until now had been ambiguous.

'I have so little time,' Craig said to himself, not realising that he had spoken aloud until his Valet replied:

'You're not late, Sir, and anyway, few people are punctual in Monte Carlo.'

Craig suddenly made up his mind.

'Go and find out what is on at the Theatre tonight!' he ordered, and his Valet hurried from the room to obey him.

He came back to say that there was an Opera, *'Faust'*, and Bellini was performing in it.

Because the singer in question was very popular Craig was quite sure the Baron would be present.

He therefore sent the Valet back to engage a box and find out without appearing to be too curious who was in each of the other boxes.

The man was away so long that Craig was just wondering impatiently whether he should go down to dinner and join his friends, when he appeared.

'They're very busy downstairs, Sir, but I found out what you wanted to know.'

He handed Craig a slip of paper on which was written a number of distinguished names, headed by Prince Albert of Monaco.

Craig was only looking for one, and when he saw it he smiled.

'Thank you,' he said to his man-servant and left the room.

The interior of the Theatre of Monte Carlo was pseudo-Gothic as was the blue dome overhead, with golden friezes, golden frescoes, golden shields, gold goddesses, naked golden boys, and golden Nubian slaves holding golden candelabra.

It was said that when Marie Blanc, wife of the man who had made the Casino at Monte Carlo a success in the first place, saw it, she said acidly:

'All this vulgar display of golden gilt will only serve to remind the customers how much they have lost at the tables.'

88

Nevertheless the Theatre had been a success since its inception in 1879 when Sarah Bernhardt had recited at the Gala opening.

Craig was therefore not surprised to find it packed when accompanied by his friends with whom he had dined, he entered his box just before the curtain rose.

He thought that the Opera was brilliantly done, but he was really only interested in watching the man sitting alone in the next box.

He did not have to be told that it was Baron Strogoloff for he was sitting in a wheel-chair, in which he had been half-propelled, half-carried to a position from which he could see the stage most comfortably.

The Baron looked like a large, over-grown goblin, and Craig, imagining him sitting with the Countess, thought they would be a perfect example of 'Beauty and the Beast'.

If he had gone on the stage just as he was, the Baron would have conveyed the horror that the Beast evoked in everybody he met without the need of make-up or 'props'.

Watching him, Craig noticed his claw-like hands with their large joints, the cruelty of his down-turned mouth, and the sharpness of his dark eyes which never left the stage.

Bellini may have sung brilliantly, but Craig never heard a note. He was concentrating all his powers of intuition and perception on the Baron.

When the interval came and his friends moved out of the box to talk to other people, he walked the few steps to the box next to his and opened the door.

Immediately a man sitting just inside who had been out of sight rose to his feet as if to bar his way, but quickly Craig passed him and went up to the Baron to say:

'May I introduce myself? I am Craig Vandervelt, and my yacht *'The Mermaid'* is in the harbour a few moorings away from your boat, the *'Tsarina'*. As one sea-loving man to another, I am very anxious to have a word with you.'

He knew as he spoke that the Baron was surprised, but then he said in tolerably good English:

'I have noticed your yacht, Mr. Vandervelt. I hear it is new.'

'Very new,' Craig answered, 'and as I have invented a new type of engine and some special lighting to be used at night which I believe has never been installed in a sea-going vessel before, you can imagine I am curious to know if yours can beat me in respect of any new ideas.'

He was speaking with a slightly exaggerated American accent which was at any other time indiscernable.

He also affected an eagerness and a slightly boastful bravado which he was certain the Baron would not miss.

There was a little pause. Then the Baron asked:

'What other new ideas have you incorporated in your yacht?'

Craig reeled off a number which he thought would interest and intrigue any other yachtsman and finished by saying:

'I am hoping that the American Navy will adopt some of these inventions.'

'This all sounds very interesting, Mr. Vandervelt,' the Baron said at length.

'What I am going to ask, Sir, though it may sound a little pushing,' Craig said with a deprecating laugh, 'is whether you would like to come aboard the *'Mermaid'* and then show me the *'Tsarina'*. To tell you the truth, I have never been aboard a Russian ship.'

'You will find it very old-fashioned,' the Baron said dryly. 'Russians are not very receptive to new ideas.'

'That is not your reputation now, Sir,' Craig replied, 'either personally or as a country. We in America have been told that Russia is surging ahead when it comes to ships and guns, and it is about time we looked to our reputation! After all we invented the Clipper!'

'That is true,' the Baron agreed. 'Well, Mr. Vandervelt, I shall be pleased to welcome you aboard the. *'Tsarina'* tomorrow.'

'What I suggest, Baron,' Craig said eagerly, 'is that you have luncheon with me on the *'Mermaid'* and afterwards show me the *'Tsarina'*.'

'I am pleased to accept your invitation, Mr. Vandervelt,' the Baron replied. 'You will not object if I bring two of my friends with me?'

'No, of course not,' Craig smiled. 'The more, the merrier.'

He was quite certain from the note in the Baron's voice that the men he brought with him would be technicians who could copy anything that interested them.

The Orchestra had returned and the Conductor reappeared to a burst of applause.

'That is a date, Sir!' Craig said rising and holding out his hand. 'I will expect you at one o'clock, and I am mighty glad to have made your acquaintance.'

He shook the Baron's hand heartily and returned to his own box.

He was conscious as he did so that his luck had once again not failed him, and as he had touched the Baron's hand with his he could understand only too well why the Countess was afraid.

CHAPTER FIVE

On leaving the Theatre with his party, they inevitably went to the Casino, and walked through the public part of it into the *Salle Touzet*, where Craig was hoping he would find the Countess.

Already the room was filled with gamblers and as his party dispersed to the various different tables he had a word with the Grand Duke and several other friends before he caught sight of the Countess.

Once again she was spectacular, wearing a gown of peacock blue which made both her skin and her hair seem dazzling, and ended round her feet in a swirl of feathers.

There was no ornamentation except one huge aquamarine, hung on a slender chain round her neck.

The effect was sensational and she seemed to stand out even in a room filled with beautiful women as if she was a light in a dark sky.

She was sitting at a table alone with Lord Neasdon and, as might have been expected, he was talking while she listened.

Because Craig thought it was a mistake to approach her too obviously he went to the Roulette table nearest to where they were sitting and pretended to watch the gamblers occasionally himself staking on a number.

He kept turning over in his mind the puzzle as to why she was so afraid, but if, as he suspected, she was under orders from the Baron it was not so surprising.

Because she seemed so fragile, so ethereal, it was somehow impossible to imagine her co-operating with a beast like Baron Strogoloff. Yet there was no doubt that she was spying for the Russians.

If it was the Baron who had taken Randall Sare prisoner, then it was quite obvious that the whole of his problem in Monte Carlo emanated from him.

Like a vast spider, Craig thought, he was spinning his web round those he had captured to entwine them like flies and it would be incredibly difficult for them to escape.

He was suddenly aware because he had been so pre-occupied with his thoughts the money he had put on number nine which was a number he often favoured and had accumulated twice, and the *Croupier* was looking at him enquiringly as to whether he would take his gains or let it run for a third time.

Almost as if he asked fortune for a sign as to whether he would win or lose a very much more complicated game than the one in front of him, Craig indicated that his gains were to remain where they were.

The *Croupier* picked up the small round ball, spun it, and said without any expression in his voice:

'*Mesdames et Monsieurs. Rien ne va plus*!'

Several greedy hands reached out in a last desperate effort to believe that fate and fortune would smile on them. Then there was the dull click as the ball came to rest.

The Croupier said still in his expressionless tones:

'*Neuf, noir et impair,*' and Craig felt sure he would be successful in the greater issue too.

He picked up what he had won amongst the envious glances of those sitting at the table, and walked to the cash-desk to change the gold coins into notes which he placed in the inside pocket of his tail-coat.

Then slowly, casually, he moved as if a magnet drew him back towards the Countess, debating whether he would speak to her, and if he did so what he would say.

He stopped on the other side of the same roulette table and now he was aware that Lord Neasdon was leaning forward, speaking urgently and undoubtedly in a more animated way than was usual.

One of the things Craig had learned when he was carrying out previous missions for the Marquess was lip-reading.

He had taken lessons from a very experienced teacher in New

93

York thinking it might at some time come in useful, although at that moment there had been no necessity for it.

He had almost forgotten that it was something at which when his lessons were finished he had become exceptionally proficient.

Almost without realising it he found he could understand what Lord Neasdon was saying, and moved a little further round the table so that he could see him practically full face.

'Stop playing games with me, Aloya! My patience is exhausted, and I will not longer be put off with promises of a tomorrow that never comes.'

The Countess's lips moved and although Craig was aware that it must have been difficult for Lord Neasdon to hear what she was saying, he knew that she replied:

'I . . I do not know what to say . . please . . could you not . . come to my . . room and perhaps . . talk to me?'

'Talk? Who wants to talk?' Lord Neasdon asked aggressively. 'I want you, Aloya, and you are driving me mad! You said yourself that we were made for each other! It is inevitable that you must be mine.'

'I . . I hoped,' the Countess said and her lips were trembling, 'that you would be . . kind to me.'

'Kind?' Lord Neasdon asked. 'Of course I want to be kind to you, but as a man I also want you and I have played your game long enough. Either let me love you tonight, or I will realise I am just being made a fool of, and will leave Monte Carlo tomorrow.'

The Countess gave a little cry which Craig knew was one of fear.

'Oh, no . . you must . . not do that! I want you to stay . . you must stay!'

There was a complacent smile on Lord Neasdon's face as he said:

'Then what are we arguing about, my dear? I will make you very happy, and tomorrow we will go to Cartier and I will buy you something beautiful to commemorate the beginning of what I know will be a long and very exciting relationship.'

The way he spoke, the expression in his eyes, and the smile on his lips made Craig feel a sudden fury which brought the blood throbbing into his head.

Only the rigid self-control which he had exercised over the years prevented him from going to the table and knocking Lord Neasdon down.

Then surprised by the violence of his feelings, he suddenly knew that he was in love as he had never been in love before!

Because it was so amazing he could not for the moment credit that he was not imagining it.

He knew that he wanted to protect the Countess, not only from Lord Neasdon, but from everything that was frightening her and making her tremble.

Never in his long experience with women who had pursued him and with whom he had been infatuated to the point of being a most ardent lover, had he felt as he felt now.

What was so astonishing was that it was for a woman whom he should have regarded with contempt as a spy for the Russians and a danger to everything he had fought for and risked his life for in the past.

'I love her!' he said to himself in wonderment, and knew it was true.

There was nothing he could do until the situation became clearer than it was at the moment. But before he could rescue her from a brute like the Baron, he must first prevent Lord Neasdon from doing what he intended tonight.

Almost as if he was being guided he knew the answer to the first step, if nothing else.

He walked towards the table and as he reached it said in a deliberately light tone:

'I thought I should find you here, but I wish you had been with me at the tables a few minutes ago when my lucky number came up three times running.'

As he spoke with a smile he realised the Countess was looking up at him with an undoubted expression of relief in her strange eyes, while Lord Neasdon was obviously finding it difficult not to show resentment at his intrusion.

'I suppose,' Craig went on, 'I must celebrate my win in the usual manner. Will you have a glass of champagne with me?'

'We have some already,' Lord Neasdon said in quite a surly tone.

'Oh, so you have!' Craig exclaimed, looking at the wine-cooler beside his chair. 'So perhaps I should find our host of last night who I see at the other side of the room and thank him for a most enjoyable evening.'

'I should do that,' Lord Neasdon said.

Craig made as if to leave the table, then he turned back.

'By the way, Countess,' he said, 'I am hoping you will not be disturbed tonight.'

'Disturbed?' she asked in a hesitating little voice, speaking for the first time since he had joined them.

'I have just heard that the Rajah of Pudakota is giving a party in his Suite at the *Hôtel de Paris*. I do not know which floor you are on, but the Rajah's parties are usually very noisy.'

'I am . . on the . . third floor.'

'I have a feeling, although I hope I am wrong,' Craig went on, 'that is the same as the Rajah's.'

He paused for a moment. Then he said with feigned anger:

'I cannot think why people give parties in the hotel where they are staying. They have no consideration for their fellow-guests. If I am at all disturbed, I am going to make a very strong protest to the Manager tomorrow morning, and I hope, Countess, you will do the same.'

'Y . . yes . . I will . . if I am . . disturbed.'

'I do not imagine His Highness will have a Band,' Craig continued, 'but there will undoubtedly be people coming and going half the night and talking at the tops of their voices in the corridors as if nobody else exists.'

'It sounds . . very . . disturbing,' the Countess said faintly.

'It will be, I assure you,' Craig said grimly, 'but I am afraid there is nothing we can do about it until it happens.'

'No . . of course not.'

He turned to the sullen nobleman and added:

'You are lucky, Neasdon, to be at the *Hermitage*. Next time I come to Monte Carlo I think I shall try it. The trouble with the *Hôtel de Paris* is that it is too popular.'

He did not wait for Lord Neasdon to reply but smiled at

the Countess as he said:

'Goodnight, but I am afraid I am being optimistic in thinking we have little chance of it being anything but a bad one.'

He laughed as if at his own joke, and moved away crossing the room to where he could see the Grand Duke smoking a large cigar and talking to Zsi-Zsi.

He could only pray that after what he had said Lord Neasdon would be too nervous to force his way into the Countess's room and at least for tonight she would be undisturbed.

He talked to the Grand Duke and Zsi-Zsi for some time, deliberately standing with his back to the two people he had just left.

Then as if he felt in need of air he went out onto the terrace thinking the night air would cool his brain as well as his body.

He walked to the stone balustrade to look down at the harbour.

He could see the lights of the two Russian yachts very clearly and he could also see the 'Mermaid' some moorings away from them.

The moonlight invested the promontory with the Palace above it and the sea shimmering away to the horizon with an enchantment that was like music that lifted the heart.

There was the scent of mimosa and night-scented stock, while the stars seemed to gleam, Craig thought, like the Countess's eyes.

He knew that their beauty was like the feelings within his heart, which he still questioned because they were so improbable and unpredictable.

But he knew irrefutably that what he felt was love, and because it was not in the least like anything he had felt before his instinct recognised it, and it was something he could not deny.

'She is beautiful, desirable as a woman, and that is what I feel about her,' he tried to tell himself, but he knew he lied.

The feelings surging within him were as intimate and genuine as the power he knew he could call on in an emergency, and which had guided him ever since he had first been aware of it long ago in India.

He knew it was the same power that Randall Sare believed in and almost without being aware of it he sent out his thoughts and

97

vibrations to the man he now knew was a prisoner on one of the yachts he could see below him.

As he had said to the Countess, the transference of thought was something in which every Indian believed and which they were taught by their Gurus.

He was aware now that he knew where Sare was that he could reach him, sustain him, give him hope, and by a miracle be able to rescue him.

'Help me,' he pleaded. 'You have been in this game longer than I have, and you must tell me what to do.'

He knew as he spoke the words in his mind and sent them speeding out into the night that they came from the Life Force within him, and that he would surely get some response.

Then as he waited, almost as if there was a voice from Heaven, he knew the answer. It was there in his mind as if somebody was telling him what he should do, and all that remained was to carry out his instructions.

Just for a moment Craig felt as if the very air around him was filled with invisible wings and that, while he could not see or hear them, every instinct in his body was acutely aware of them.

Then as he tried to grasp at what he was feeling they were gone, but the plan was still there and that was all that mattered.

He had had the same experience before when he had been in a tight corner, and on one occasion on the very edge of destruction, but not so vividly nor so completely as now in reaching Randall Sare who had responded.

He stood on the terrace for a long time thinking, until aware his body was feeling the chill of the night he went back into the over-heated gaming room.

He saw as he entered that the table at which the Countess and Lord Neasdon had been sitting was now empty, and as his anxiety for her returned he felt his fists clench at the thought that Neasdon might be forcing himself upon her against her will.

He found it impossible to stay any longer in the Casino and moved without hurrying down the room, stopping at table after table so that he could be seen speaking to a man here, a lovely lady there. Then finally and unobtrusively he faded away without anybody being particularly aware of it.

98

He walked across the Square where fairy-lights were twinkling and up the steps through the brilliantly lighted door of the *Hôtel de Paris*.

He went up to his own floor, finding it quiet and with nobody in sight. He hoped therefore that the Countess had not allowed Lord Neasdon to escort her to the door of her Suite, in which case he would have been aware that there was no party taking place on that floor.

Craig went into his own rooms and because his valet was waiting for him, undressed as he always did with his help.

Then when he was wearing a long dark robe he settled himself in a comfortable chair with the latest edition of *'The Menton and Monte Carlo News'*.

This was a newspaper which was first published in 1897. From a modest four pages it had developed into twenty-eight or more and was now the main source of information on the Social life, sport and entertainment of the Principality.

It also listed the new arrivals at the hotels or Villas at which they were staying.

As he turned over the pages his valet said:

'I see, Sir, there's a lot more important guests arrived today.'

Craig made a sound of annoyance.

'There are too many people here already,' he said, 'and I think we might be more comfortable and certainly quieter aboard the *'Mermaid'*.

The valet looked depressed and Craig was aware that both the men he had brought with him preferred it when their master was ashore, finding the unpredictability of the sea something which inevitably interfered with their duties.

Then as the valet was tidying the room he added:

'Pack my clothes first thing tomorrow morning in case I decide to run down the coast for a day or so. If I change my mind they can always be unpacked.'

'Very good, Sir,' the valet replied in a voice that conveyed no enthusiasm at the idea.

Craig waited until he was alone, then putting down the newspaper he rose and locked the door of his bedroom which led into the passage, and opened the door into his Sitting-Room.

He passed through it and into the empty room on the other side. Switching on only one light, he crossed to the door which communicated with the Countess.

As he put out his hand to open the door he had unlocked previously, he knew that he was holding his breath in case he should hear Lord Neasdon's voice, then mocked, at himself.

In the past he had not only never felt jealous about a woman, but he had laughed at the men who suffered in that way.

Yet he knew now that if he heard Neasdon with the Countess he would, whatever the consequences, throw him violently out of her room and save her, as he knew she wished to be saved.

As the door opened there was only silence. Then with a leap of his heart he saw something white beneath the door.

He bent down and picked up the piece of paper and saw written in a writing which he knew expressed her personality:

'Please, I must speak to you.'

As he read the words he felt not only relief, but a feeling of indescribable happiness that she wanted him and needed him.

Quickly and skilfully he managed with the instrument he had concealed in the pocket of his robe to open the door, and as he heard the lock click into place, he knocked very gently.

Instantly, so that he knew she must have been waiting for him, she pulled it open.

There was only one light in her room, and silhouetted against it she seemed to Craig like a vision that had always been in his imagination and, although he had not been aware of it, in a special shrine in his heart.

She was wearing a white negligée which flowed softly around her, and her hair was loose, falling pale silver so that it seemed to be part of the moonlight over her shoulders and down her back almost to her waist.

For a moment they just stood staring at each other as if they had met across eternity and found each other after a very long time.

Then – and afterwards, Craig could never remember how it happened – either she or he moved, his arms were round her, and her face was hidden against his shoulder.

He could feel she was trembling, at the same time as he was

100

holding her, he knew it was the most perfect thing that had ever happened to him and was what he had sought but never found.

There was no need for words, for their closeness told them all they needed was to be together.

Then the Countess said in a whisper that was hardly audible:

'Help me . . please . . help me . . I do not know . . what to do . . and I am so desperately afraid!'

As she spoke he could feel the fear surging through her and her whole body was trembling almost uncontrollably.

He tightened his arms, knowing instinctively that the strength of them was what she needed and said very quietly:

'I am here and there is no need for you to be frightened.'

He heard the Countess draw in her breath, and he went on:

'I think you would be happier and more sure that no-one could hear what you have to tell me if you come into my Sitting-Room.'

She raised her head then, and looked towards the outer door and he thought he had never seen such terror in any woman's eyes, and that if it cost him his life, he would somehow save her as she had asked him to do.

She made no reply and he pulled her gently through the door he had just opened, closing it behind them.

He drew her across the empty room and into his Sitting-Room where there were shaded lights, flowers and his personal things scattered around which made it somehow seem a haven of security.

He did not take his arm from her, but drew her towards a comfortable sofa. Then before he sat down he looked down at her, thinking how lovely she was and at the same time with her hair falling over her shoulders she looked very young, little more than a girl.

She looked up at him and he felt she was questioning whether she was right to be where she was and close to him, but knew it was something she could not help.

'I told you to trust me,' he said very gently, 'and now there is a very good reason why you should do so.'

He did not wait for her to ask what it was, but added:

'I love you! I was aware of it just now when I saw what was happening in the Casino, and because I love you I swear I will

101

save you and you shall never again be as frightened as you are now.'

She made an inarticulate little sound and her eyes filled with tears. Slowly Craig bent his head and very gently his lips found hers.

He kissed her because he could not help himself. At the same time, while he loved her he did not desire her passionately, but somehow spiritually because she was part of the vibrations he had felt outside the Casino and the power he had evoked within himself on her behalf as well as from Randall Sare.

Then as he felt her lips quiver beneath his and he found they were innocent, inexperienced and very soft, his kiss became more insistent, more demanding, and he pulled her still closer to him.

He was aware as he did so that this kiss was different from any other he had ever given or received in the past.

He could not explain it, he only knew that she had walked into his heart she was a part of him, and now and for all time she was his.

Only when he felt they were one with the stars and the moon, and at the same time enveloped by a glory that was not of this world, did he raise his head and she said in a whisper he could hardly hear:

'I love . . you! I did not . . know I . . loved you . . and yet I have thought . . about . . you ever since we . . first met.'

'You thought of me – in what way?' Craig asked in a voice that was very deep.

'I knew you were the . . only person I could trust when . . everything else was . . horrifying and . . evil.'

'And now you know that what you felt was love.'

'I love you . . I love . . you . . and I ought not to bring you into this . . ghastly situation which is . . very dangerous . . but there is no one . . else to whom I can . . turn.'

'You must tell me all about it, my darling,' Craig said, 'but first I must kiss you again and because we love each other we will find a solution to your problem. I know it!'

He kissed her until he was aware that she had forgotten her fear and what she was feeling was something very different. As

102

her body quivered against his, he knew it was from the rapture of love and the sensations which he gave her were ones she had never experienced before.

Then as he drew her down onto the sofa he said in a voice which was strangely unsteady:

'There is one thing I must know before anything else – are you really married?'

'No . . no . . it was just . . part of the . . disguise.'

His relief made him feel as if the whole room was suddenly lit with a celestial light and he said as if he must make certain of the truth:

'And you have never been kissed?'

'Only . . by you.'

'My darling, I was sure of it when I touched your lips, and now I understand why, if no man has possessed you, you could not allow Neasdon to touch you.'

The Countess gave a little cry.

'You . . saved me . . tonight. He was too . . afraid to come upstairs when you said there was a . . party on this floor, but . . they will be . . very angry . . because they told me . . .'

She stopped and as if she was afraid to say any more she hid her face against Craig's shoulder.

'They told you what?' he asked, 'and I know now who you are speaking of – the Russians!'

The shudder that ran through her confirmed his words and she said after a moment:

'If I do not . . allow Lord Neasdon to . . become my . . lover . . they have said that they will take Papa away to Russia . . and I shall never . . see him again.'

Craig stiffened. Then he said:

'Your father? You cannot be Randall Sare's daughter!'

As he spoke he thought he had been very obtuse not to have realised this before.

Aloya raised her head.

'You . . know Papa?'

'Of course I know him, although I have only just learnt that the reason for his disappearance is that the Russians have him aboard the Baron's yacht.'

She turned to him questioningly. Then she asked:

'H. .how can you. .know this? How can you be. .aware of it. . when it is not known to . . anybody else in Monte Carlo?'

Craig's arms tightened around her as he said:

'There are a lot of explanations to be made, but first I want to hear about everything that has happened to you. Then I will explain why I am here.'

'It is a reason that . . concerns Papa?'

'Yes.'

She gave a little cry.

'Now I know why I was so sure that . . you would help me. I felt sure there was something about you that was different from anyone . . else!'

Her eyes were shining as she said:

'Papa has always told me to trust in my intuition and he was right.'

'Of course he was right,' Craig said, 'and that is why I felt that you were not what you pretended to be.'

She gave a little sigh and he said:

'It is hard to express how glad I am that you are not the Countess Aloya Zladamir.'

'It was the name they gave me,' Aloya said, 'because it sounded impressive, and they thought Lord Neasdon would find it easier to spend his time with a married woman than with a young girl, because of course as a girl I should have a proper chaperon.'

'I understand their reasoning, although I suppose it was the Baron who thought out the somewhat complicated plot.'

'Y. .yes. .the. .Baron! He is. .wicked. .evil! If Satan is a man . . then he is the Baron!' Aloya said passionately.

'Were you with your father when he was captured by them?'

As if she knew she must tell him the whole story Aloya put her head on Craig's shoulder. At the same time she drew a little closer to him and his arms tightened around her.

Because he cold not help himself he kissed her forehead. Then he said:

'Start from the beginning. I had no idea, and nor has anybody in England, that Randall Sare is a married man.'

104

'He kept it a secret because he thought that those who trusted him would find it hard to continue to do so if he had a wife who was what they thought of as a Russian.'

Craig asked her to explain and she said:

'Mama is actually Georgian, and my grandfather, Prince Volvershi was very important in Georgia before it was annexed by the Russians.'

Craig knew only too well how this had happened, but he did not interrupt and Aloya went on:

'Mama fell in love with Papa when he came to Georgia, intending to move from there into Afghanistan, to find out what was being planned for rousing the tribesmen against the British.'

She smiled as she said:

'He loved Mama the moment he saw her, and they knew that nobody else would ever be of any importance to either of them.'

'That is how I feel about you.'

'And it is the way I love you,' Aloya answered. 'I have a always prayed that I would find a man to whom I could belong, and Mama knew as soon as she saw Papa that he had always been in her dreams.'

Craig kissed her forehead again, but he knew he must hear the whole story and Aloya continued:

'In spite of my grandfather's opposition, they were married very quietly and secretly because as Papa explained, the Foreign Office in England and those who trusted him in India would not understand that the nationality of his wife would not interfere with his work for them.'

She made a little gesture with her hands before she said:

'No one who comes from Georgia thinks of themselves as Russian, although we dare not say so if they are listening.'

'I know that.'

'Because Mama had no wish to spoil Papa's life which he loved, and in which he was so useful to those with whom he worked, she never interfered.'

She paused before she went on:

'After I was born at home in Georgia, we joined him whenever it was possible, sometimes in strange places on the plains of

India, sometimes in the foothills of the Himalayas, or in dak bungalows where we would go for days, sometimes weeks, without seeing anybody.'

Craig understood now where Randall Sare had been many of the times when he had disappeared and no one had any news of him.

'Then Papa would have another assignment,' Aloya said, 'or a message from those in authority, and usually he would send us home, or we would go to one of the big towns like Bombay or Calcutta, and live there very quietly so that nobody paid any attention to us, or had any idea that we even existed.'

'A very strange life!' Craig remarked.

'Fortunately we had plenty of money and Papa was insistent that I should be well educated and have the very best teachers available. When he was at home he taught me his own beliefs, and that is the only reason why I have not been more frantic about him than I am at the moment . . but time is running out.'

'What do you mean by that?' Craig asked.

'I think you will understand where most people would not,' Aloya said, 'but when we were captured by the Russians here in Monte Carlo . . .'

'Wait a minute!' Craig interrupted. 'You are going too fast. First of all, why did he come home? He told me he would never return to England.'

'Oh . . of course . . I forgot to tell you,' Aloya said. 'Mama . . died! She had not been well for some time, but I managed with difficulty to send for Papa, and he was there to say . . goodbye to her.'

Her voice trembled for a moment. Then she said, and it was very moving:

'Mama knew he was coming and hung on, and hung on when she might otherwise have died . . until he actually appeared.'

She turned her face against Craig's neck and he knew she was crying as she said:

'She . . just had . . time to tell Papa how much she . . loved him and how . . happy he had . . made her . . then her spirit slipped away . . and there was only her . . body left behind.'

Craig held Aloya very closely as he said:

106

'I know that describes what happened, but she must be still near you, to tell you that you can trust me.'

'Of course she is . . and near Papa . . and although he would not . . mind dying . . I can not . . lose him.'

'He would be a loss to the whole world,' Craig said. 'But tell me why he was coming back to England.'

'It was . . because he could not . . leave me alone in India, and although I begged him not to do so he decided to take me to his sister with whom he has always kept in touch. He thought she would not only look after me, but would introduce me to English Society.'

Aloya paused before she said:

'He decided it was quite straightforward until he realised that the Russians were determined because he had returned from Tibet to either capture . . or kill him.'

'You were not in Tibet with him?' Craig asked incredulously.

'We only went as far as Gangtse just inside the country. We had a house there while Papa went wandering about, finding out from the monasteries and of course in Lhasa, what the British wanted to know.'

Aloya paused for a moment before she said:

'When Mama died in Gangtse there was nothing Papa could do but come home.'

'Which of course was quite right where you were concerned.'

'I do not think so, but I always do what Papa wants.'

'What I cannot understand is why you left the ship at Nice and came here,' Craig said.

'We went on board in disguise,' Aolya said. 'In fact Papa was a Turk, and nobody questioned for a moment that he was anything other than he appeared to be.'

And you?'

'I was his wife! I wore a *yashmak* and a *burnous* which as you are aware is very concealing. One can be fat, thin, pretty or ugly, and nobody would be any the wiser.'

'A very good thing, as you are so very lovely, my darling.'

Aloya drew in her breath.

'I want you to . . think that.'

'I will tell you exactly what I think when you have finished

107

your story. Why did you get off the ship in the South of France?'

'We were quite certain that no one on board had the slightest idea that Papa was not the Turk he pretended to be, but when we stopped at Naples for new passengers to come on board, among them were two men whom Papa recognised and he thought they recognised him too.'

Craig heard the fear in her voice as she went on:

'It was not however until we reached Nice that he was sure they intended to kill him. We slipped ashore the moment the ship docked, leaving behind practically everything we possessed so that they would not be suspicious until after the ship had left harbour.'

Craig saw the reasoning behind this and Aloya went on:

'Papa did not know where we could be safe in Nice, but there was a place he knew in Monte Carlo and we went there.'

She gave a little sigh as she added:

'It was rather scruffy and uncomfortable. I went out shopping for our food, and although I did not see anybody about who seemed in the least suspicious, Papa's instinct told him that he must not take any risks.'

Craig knew they must have been hiding in the place where Father Augustin had made enquiries in the first place.

'Why did you leave?' he asked.

'It was very unfortunate,' Aloya replied, 'but a man who was also in hiding came to this particular place, and Papa recognised him as an informer who would give information to anybody who was willing to pay for it, and it was therefore too dangerous for us to stay.'

'So you moved,' Craig said, 'and that was disastrous.'

'How do you know?' Aloya enquired. 'What happened was that we left where we were really safe and Papa instructed me to walk on the other side of the street from him.'

Craig realised this was when he must have been seen by one of the British agents.

'He turned the corner along a street,' Aloya said, 'and there were two men waiting for him who seized him, and he had no chance to escape from them.'

'What did you do?'

'What could I do?' she asked. 'I did not have time to reason it out. I just ran to Papa to be with him, for whatever happened we would be together.'

The way she spoke was very moving and Craig said:

'I understand, and so they took both you and your father to the Baron.'

'It was . . terrifying,' Aloya said. 'They started to question Papa, and when he refused to tell them anything they wanted they said they would take him back to Russia, and . . torture him until he . . told them what they . . wanted to hear.'

Craig knew from the way she spoke how terrifying it had been.

'Then Papa said he would tell them some of the things they wanted to know if they would let me go free.'

She gave a deep sigh.

'That was a great mistake. The Baron looked at me as if he saw me for the first time, and I knew by the expression in his eyes that he thought I might be useful to them.'

'So it was the Baron who thought up the idea that you should seduce Lord Neasdon into revealing his secrets about Tibet?'

'He told me he was very, very important to the Foreign Office and would know the British plans if the Russians should invade that country.'

'So they dressed you up in spectacular fashion!'

'They told me exactly what I was to do,' Aloya said with a shudder.

'And your clothes?'

'A French designer over whom they apparently had some hold was brought to the yacht and instructed to make me look outstanding so that it would be impossible for Lord Neasdon not to notice me.'

'But surely he was not expected to speak to you on sight?' Craig asked, feeling it was somehow out of character considering Neasdon's impression of his own importance.

'Oh, no,' Aloya cried, 'they were far too clever for that! They found out all about him. His mother, of whom he is very fond, was leaving the day after he arrived here for America,

109

and by some method of their own they obtained a letter she had written.'

She paused and then went on:

'I think it was to a friend of hers in Monte Carlo, and they forged her hand-writing in a letter they wrote in her name to Lord Neasdon begging him when he arrived in Monte Carlo to be kind to the daughter of somebody to whom she owed a great debt of gratitude.'

'That was you, I presume?'

'Of course, and because of the urgency with which the letter was written Lord Neasdon called on me within a few hours of his arrival.'

'And was obviously bowled over by your beauty!' Craig said cynically.

'I had to tell him how much he impressed me and how wonderful I thought he was,' Aloya said in a low voice, 'and I knew all the time I was talking to him that my maid, who of course was their spy, listened at the door to make sure I did not say . . anything that might make him . . suspicious.'

She made a little sound of despair as she said:

'How could I dare to do . . that when they had told me that if I did not do exactly as they . . wanted they would . . kill Papa immediately they had extracted his secrets from him?'

'Is that what they have been doing in the meantime?' Craig asked anxiously.

'No, Papa has been too clever for them,' Aloya replied. 'He played for time while they were arranging my clothes and the Baron was lending me the jewels I wore which of course are his. Then when they began to question him seriously he went into a trance.'

'A trance?' Craig exclaimed.

'It is something he learnt to do in India, and he can render himself completely unconscious so that it is impossible to waken him. But naturally the trance only lasts for a certain time.'

'How long?' Craig asked, knowing it was of vital importance.

'Unless he is to die for lack of food and water,' Aloya said in a voice that trembled, 'he has . . to come back to . . consciousness . . tomorrow!'

Craig knew then that was why he had been aware perceptively that the sands of time were running out and that he had to do something quickly.

He was not only afraid for Aloya but in some special way Randall Sare had made him aware that there was no more time.

'The Russians do not know this,' he said, 'so why did they say you had to take Lord Neasdon as your lover tonight?'

'They are waiting for Papa to regain consciousness and for me to give them results. Then they intend to take both of us away, and if I have nothing to tell them . . I think they will . . torture me in front of Papa to make him speak.'

Craig thought this was very likely, and he said angrily:

'I swear to you, my darling, that shall not happen as long as I am alive.'

'Can you . . save Papa . . and me?'

'I swear I will do so,' he said, 'and I know you will believe me as no one else would when I tell you that tonight when I was on the terrace outside the Casino I was told either by your father or some other force what I have to do.'

He saw Aloya look up at him and the expression in her eyes told him she not only believed him, but knew he would succeed.

Then, as if there was no more to say, his lips were on hers and he kissed her, masterfully, possessively, passionately, not as if she was a shy young girl, but a woman whom he loved more than anything else in the whole world.

CHAPTER SIX

Craig awoke with a feeling of happiness which for the moment made him forget the difficult, dangerous task which lay ahead.

All he could think of was his love for Aloya, how last night he had held her in his arms and known that she was everything he needed to make himself complete and that he was the most fortunate man in the whole world.

Having travelled in so many lands and having done so many strange things in his life, he was aware she was unique, not only in her astounding beauty, but in the intelligence of her mind, her quickness of thought, and most of all her intuition and perception which was the same as his own.

Her beauty, he now realised, came from her mixture of blood in which she combined the fair skin of her English forebears with the mystical beauty of her Russian eyes.

It was this ancestry which had added the strange silver sheen to her hair which Craig realised he had occasionally seen before on Russian women, whose hair however had been black.

He also knew, and he was certain that it was something Aloya believed, as her father did, that when two people loved each other overwhelmingly and were in fact the spiritual counterpart of each other, their children had a beauty that was created by love itself.

He knew better than most men the difficulties Randall Sare must have encountered when he had been forced because of his work to keep his marriage a secret from everybody.

It was not only, Craig was sure, because the authorities

would have been shocked at his marrying a woman who was ostensibly Russian, but also because his enemies might, as they were doing now, use his wife and family as a weapon against him.

It was still hard to credit that Aloya and her mother had travelled over the bitterly cold, treacherous and extremely dangerous Pass which connected India with Tibet.

But he had known that Gangtse, the first town inside the forbidden territory, was a Trading Post, and therefore they would not have aroused as much interest or hostility as they would have done further into the country.

Then in the dim light as the dawn crept up the sky Craig thought that only Randall Sare would have felt it obligatory to leave his wife and daughter in such a strange place and go off into the blue, disguised so cleverly that he must have convinced everybody he met that he was neither a spy nor an enemy.

This might be comparatively easy in India or other countries in the East, but the Tibetans had a perception equal to his own.

Some of the older Monks in the great Monasteries could use what the uninitiated thought was clairvoyance or magic, but which in fact was a supernormal power to find the truth.

Craig could understand how Sare, bereft of his wife whom he loved so deeply and encumbered with a very beautiful daughter, had known that the only possible thing he could do was to take her to England and safety.

And yet, because of his reputation and because to the Russians he was a marked man, they were both now in a situation which Craig knew was so dangerous and so desperate that one false step could destroy them both.

The thought of losing Aloya was like a thousand daggers striking at his heart, and he made up his mind quite calmly and positively that if she died, he would die with her.

'I would have bet my entire fortune,' he told himself with a twist of his lips, 'that no woman could ever have made me feel as I feel now, but I know now that every word the poets ever wrote about love and every note the musicians played was true.'

Then he forced himself not to think of the emotions surging within his heart, but to concentrate his brain and his whole

113

being on what lay ahead.

Last night when he had taken Aloya to the door of her bedroom he had said:

'From this moment leave everything in my hands. Trust me, pray, and send out the vibrations which we both know will be received by your father.'

'Will you be doing . . that?' Aloya asked.

'You know I will,' Craig replied. 'I shall be telling him to be prepared, and I know he will understand.'

He thought as he spoke there was no other woman in the whole world to whom he could say such things.

He had then held her close in his arms and kissed her passionately and demandingly until they were both breathless with their hearts beating frantically against each other's.

'I love you,' Craig said hoarsely, 'and love will always win.'

'You are . . sure of . . that?'

'Look at me!' he commanded masterfully.

She did as he told her and he thought no woman could look more lovely or more desirable, and their need of each other was like the air they breathed and the sunshine which came from the sky.

Then as her eyes were held by his he saw the fear, the worry and anxiety being replaced by a rapture which ran through him like little streaks of lightning, and he knew she was feeling the same.

Because there were no words to express what they were both feeling he kissed her again, and since words were superfluous, without saying any more, he shut the doors between them and went to his own room.

Now he was going over step by step in his mind exactly what must be done, trying to make every detail foolproof as he had been taught to do in the past, anticipating the worst and being prepared for it, obeying the golden rule which was never to take an unnecessary chance.

Nobody who saw him a little later walking through the *Hôtel de Paris* to the Tennis Courts which were behind it and in front of the *Hermitage* would have guessed that he had anything on his mind but the joy of Spring and an anticipation of hard

114

exercise to sweep away the excesses of the night before.

The Pro. was waiting for him and as usual Craig managed to beat him in the last set, and they arranged to play again the following morning.

After he had put on his thick woollen sweater he walked not back to the *Hôtel de Paris*, but to the *Hermitage*, passing through the glass door he went to the Reception Desk.

'Is Lord Neasdon down yet?' he asked. 'I would like to have a word with him.'

The Receptionist smiled at him in recognition.

'Good morning, Mr. Vandervelt, His Lordship is in the Breakfast Room. Shall I tell him you are here?'

'I will speak to him myself,' Craig replied.

He walked into the Breakfast Room thinking it was typically English of Lord Neasdon to breakfast downstairs rather than in his own Suite.

There were only a few other people in the room, and a glance showed him that Lord Neasdon was sitting at a table in the window reading the newspaper.

Craig walked to his table and only when he had stood for a second waiting did Lord Neasdon raise his head.

'Good morning, Vandervelt,' he said in a not particularly effusive tone. 'You are very early.'

'I am sorry to disturb you,' Craig replied, 'but I am hoping that you will join me for luncheon aboard my yacht the *'Mermaid'* today. I am having a small party, and I am very anxious for both you and the Countess to see my new yacht.'

He knew as he finished speaking that Lord Neasdon was wondering how he could refuse because he disliked him, but before he could say anything Craig went on:

'I have already sent a note to the Countess, and I hope you will bring her with you in my motor car, which will be outside the *Hôtel de Paris* at one o'clock.'

There was really nothing Lord Neasdon could do in the circumstances but accept, and as he did so, somewhat ungraciously, Craig said:

'That is splendid! I shall look forward to seeing you. Goodbye until then, and perhaps we might take a turn out to sea after luncheon if the weather is as good as it is now.'

He was gone before Lord Neasdon could think of a reply, and there was a smile of satisfaction on his lips as he walked back to his hotel.

Because he thought it would be a mistake for him not to do everything he normally did, he spent the next two hours in his Sitting Room writing letters with his secretary and paying bills, until soon after noon he walked onto the terrace.

The usual friends were congregated there, and he found Zsi-Zsi and the Grand Duke entertaining a number of people.

He joined them and received several invitations which he accepted, until at exactly half past twelve he left the terrace and was driven in his car down to the harbour.

His secretary had already carried out his instructions to alert the 'Mermaid', and as he came aboard the Captain said:

'Everything's prepared, Sir, and I hope to your liking. The Chef complained it was rather short notice, but I don't think you will be disappointed in the menu.'

'I am sure I will not be,' Craig replied. 'And now, Captain, I want a word with you, so we will go into the Saloon.'

The Saloon, which was painted pale green and had very attractive chintz covers over the furniture which matched the curtains, was a novelty in the yachting world, which up to now had kept strictly to the traditional polished mahogany panelling and leather chairs.

Having shut the door the Captain stood waiting for his orders which Craig gave him, slowly and clearly, making absolutely certain they were understood.

Only after he had finished speaking did the Captain give a little gasp and say;

'It seems almost incredible, Sir!'

'I agree with you,' Craig said, 'but when I engaged you, Captain, I went very carefully into your background, and I know you have been through some traumatic experiences of your own, and carried out your orders with a heroism which should have been rewarded.'

The Captain looked almost bashful.

'It's very kind of you to say so, Sir.'

116

'You will understand after what I have told you,' Craig said, 'that this is the reason I chose an Englishman to command my yacht, although I am in fact an American.'

'That's a compliment I greatly appreciate,' the Captain replied.

'Then brief your men, Captain, and let there be absolutely no mistakes. The timing has to be done to a split second.'

'I understand, Sir.'

He saluted smartly and Craig was aware that there was a look of admiration in his eyes which had never been there before.

It amused him to think how in the past while the Captain had been prepared to command his ship and obey his orders to the letter it had always been at the back of his mind that it was a pity he was an American.

It was something he had met before with the English, and when he was engaged on some desperate mission on their behalf he often longed to damn their impertinence for daring to think because he belonged to another nation he was not only slightly inferior, but less intelligent than they were.

There was however no time for personal retrospect.

Instead Craig went from the Saloon into the smaller room adjacent to it which was where they were to eat.

This room was also decorated in green, but the seats and the chairs and curtains were not of chintz, but of an emerald green velvet which was echoed in the leaves of the camelias which decorated the table.

The centre-piece was a silver galleon made in Venice in the 16th century and the rest of the silver was early Georgian. Craig wondered if his guests would appreciate the time and thought he had given to the furnishings of the *Mermaid*.

Because he could afford it he wanted everything to be superlative of its kind as well as in excellent taste, and he had only to look at the very fine oil paintings of ships which decorated the walls to know there was no yacht afloat that carried such treasures.

In the silver ice-bucket there was champagne and also wines of excellent vintages from the finest vineyards in France.

As Craig stood looking at them his head steward came in

looking exceedingly smart in his silver-buttoned white cut-away coat.

Craig gave him his orders which like those he had given to the Captain were concise, clear and impossible to misunderstand.

Then when the steward, who had been with him for some years in his other yachts, showed that he understood what was required, Craig moved back into the Saloon.

Exactly at the time expected, Baron Strogoloff was pushed aboard in his wheel-chair to be welcomed by Craig's secretary, Mr. Cavendish, at the top of the gangway, and brought from there into the Saloon.

He was followed by two stalwart-looking Russians, hard-faced men but dressed impeccably in yachting clothes in which they appeared somewhat out of place and ill at ease.

One glance at them before he greeted the Baron told Craig they were exactly what he had expected them to be, technicians who would take note of everything that they saw, and make sure the information was relayed to the yachts of the Russian Navy.

Smiling and speaking affably he held out his hand to the Baron saying:

'I am delighted to see you, Baron, and I have so much to show you after luncheon.'

The Baron's wheel-chair was placed at the far end of the Saloon and after Craig had shaken hands with his two attendants and asked them to sit down the stewards immediately carried round glasses of Vodka.

The Russians swilled them down their throats in one gulp and the glasses were immediately refilled as Craig sat down beside the Baron to say with an air of boyish eagerness:

'How do you like my scheme of decoration?'

'It is certainly unusual, Mr. Vandervelt,' the Baron replied in a gutteral voice.

'I thought you would think so. I cannot tell you how hard the builders tried to argue with me and persuade me to be more traditional.'

'I see you have some fine pictures.'

'I agree with you, and it would be a disaster if we were sunk at

118

sea, but I do not think that will happen.'

'The sea can always be a risk to everybody,' the Baron said pompously.

Craig laughed.

'And so can a great many other things in life.'

His secretary opened the Saloon door.

'The Countess Aloya Zladamir, Sir, and Lord Neasdon!'

Craig got to his feet.

'Can I say how pleased I am to see you, Countess,' he asked, 'and looking more lovely than spring itself? I have a surprise for you because I think you told me you have not met your compatriot, Baron Strogoloff, whom I have persuaded also to be my guest.'

He knew as he took Aloya's hand in his that she was frightened. At the same time with what he knew was a clever piece of acting she replied:

'No, I have never met the Baron, but I have admired the beautiful yacht he owns.'

She walked across the room to shake hands with him, and Craig turned to Lord Neasdon to say:

'Welcome aboard, My Lord!'

He then introduced him to the Baron's two attendants who had risen rather awkwardly to their feet as the Countess had entered the cabin.

Aloya was standing by the Baron who was glaring at her, and yet Craig knew perceptively that fortified by her trust and belief in him, she was not afraid as she might have been.

As he joined her she exclaimed with exactly the right inflection in her voice:

'What a charming cabin and so different from what I expected.'

'That is what I want to hear,' Craig said, 'and the Baron has already said that he admires my pictures.'

'They are lovely, quite lovely!' Aloya cried, 'and I hope we shall be able to see the whole of your yacht before we leave.'

'Of course,' Craig replied. 'The State Rooms are very unusual, at least the American magazines seem to think so.

119

There is hardly one in which photographs of my yacht have not appeared.'

'I shall so look forward to seeing everything.'

Aloya was looking so lovely that Craig knew he had to be careful not to reveal both his admiration and his love when he looked at her.

It would be a mistake, he knew, to underestimate the Baron in any way, and as if what he was thinking communicated itself to Aloya she moved towards Lord Neasdon and slipped her arm through his.

'What do you think of it?' she asked.

She turned her eyes upwards as she spoke in a way which made Craig long to snatch her into his arms and forbid her ever to look at another man.

But he knew she was only carrying out his instructions, and Lord Neasdon said heavily:

'I suppose these pictures are originals, and not reproductions?'

'You insult me!' Craig replied lightly.

'I am sure there is . . nothing about Mr. Vandervelt which is not . . original.'

As Aloya spoke she refused a glass of Vodka, and accepted one of champagne.

Lord Neasdon looked surprised at the smaller glass saying:

'I do not believe I have ever drunk Vodka.'

'You must try it,' Craig answered. 'It is the traditional Russian drink when you are eating caviar, and as the Baron will tell you, stimulates the entire system.'

'Well, I suppose I must be daring,' Lord Neasdon said in a voice which showed it was the last thing he was likely to be.

He picked up the glass and was about to sip it when Aloya gave a little cry.

'No, no! That is not the right way to drink Vodka. You must pour it down your throat at one gulp. Am I not right, Baron?'

'That is right,' the Baron agreed.

He sat glowering from under his bushy eye-brows, and Craig had the feeling that he was slightly disconcerted at meeting her and was not quite sure what he should do about it.

The glasses of Vodka were filled and refilled before luncheon was announced.

Then the Baron's wheel-chair was pushed into the smaller Saloon next door and he was seated on Craig's left, while Aloya sat on his right with Lord Neasdon next to her.

The two Russians had been placed one beside the Baron and the other at the far end of the table. They sat down awkwardly making no effort to speak, but proceeded as the meal progressed to eat and drink everything that was put in front of them.

The Captain had been right when he said the Chef had made a great effort.

The food was delicious and Craig forced himself to eat but he was aware that because she was afraid, Aloya's throat was constricted and it was almost impossible for her to swallow anything.

However she was clever enough to appear to be eating and played about with the food on her plate only pushing what was left to one side just before the plates were removed for the next course.

Lord Neasdon, perfectly at his ease, ate heartily, but Craig knew that his guest not only disliked him as a man but was also envious of his possessions, and it was hard for him to respond effusively when Aloya praised everything including the camelias which decorated the table and the silver galleon in the centre of it.

'I am a collector of ships,' Craig explained, 'and because I am fond of the sea I have a great many ancient models in silver and gold, and some with precious stones.'

'How exciting!' Aloya exclaimed. 'I would love to see them.'

'I hope one day I will be able to show them to you.'

He spoke without any depth of feeling in his voice, but his heart told him that the day would come when he would not only show Aloya his treasures, but she would share them with him.

Then because he was determined to allay any suspicions the Baron might have that this was not a perfectly ordinary luncheon party he set out to be amusing and witty about Monte Carlo and his travels to other places in the world.

The way he talked made it impossible for anybody not to

laugh, and he was aware that the Baron relaxed a little as he drank a great deal, and his eyes did not seem quite so hard and suspicious, and even his hands a little less claw-like.

As if he wished to assert himself, Lord Neasdon told a long and rather boring story of an encounter with robbers in one of the high passes in Switzerland.

When he finished Craig capped it with a tale of being pursued by pirates off the coast of Malaya.

'I was fortunate,' he said, 'that at that time my yacht was considerably faster than their craft, otherwise I doubt if I should be here telling the tale.'

'It sounds very frightening!' Aloya said.

'When one is in danger,' Craig replied, 'one often has a feeling of exhilaration.'

'Why is that?' she asked.

'Because one is pitting one's brains and one's strength against another human being, and if the odds are equal it becomes a challenge to one's personality.'

'And if the . . odds are not . . equal?'

She spoke in a low voice, and Craig knew what she was thinking.

'One has to rely on the unexpected, or perhaps on a power greater than one's self, which is always available if we know how to look for it.'

He knew as he saw the expression in her eyes change that she understood what he was telling her, and because once again she was acting on his instructions she turned to Lord Neasdon to ask:

'Have you ever felt that?'

'I have always relied on myself and my brain,' he replied pompously, 'and that is why we British have been victorious in many different fields.'

'Of course,' Craig replied. 'At the same time, you are not doing so well at the moment against the Boers.'

He could not help the jibe, but as he saw Lord Neasdon stiffen and had no wish to antagonise him, he added quickly:

'But we are not going to talk politics today. This is a happy occasion, and as you are in fact my first party aboard the

122

'*Mermaid*' I want you to drink a special toast wishing her success and a safe harbour to wherever she journeys.'

'Of course we must do that!' Aloya cried clapping her hands.

As Craig was speaking the stewards had brought in fresh glasses and while one man passed them around to the guests, the other carried a decanter in each hand.

'This is the most famous wine in Europe in which to drink a toast,' Craig explained. 'It is Tokay which you all know comes from Hungary, and is highly esteemed by the Austrians, as I am sure the Baron is aware.'

'Yes, indeed,' the Baron agreed, 'but I do not think I have ever drunk Tokay.'

'Then this is the first time for you, and the first luncheon party aboard the '*Mermaid*' and the first time I have ever had such a beautiful guest as the Countess.'

Aloya looked shy and blushed, and Craig knew for the moment she was not acting.

The steward filled the glasses, then as if he could not be left out Lord Neasdon said:

'I will propose the toast! To the '*Mermaid*', to its owner, and of course to somebody who is more beautiful and more alluring than any mermaid or siren to be found in the sea!'

Looking at Aloya he raised his glass and as she smiled at him he drank down the Tokay saying as he did so:

'No heel-taps!'

It was echoed with pleasure as the Russians obeyed him and the glasses of Tokay disappeared down their throats at the same speed as the Vodka had.

'That was a very nice toast,' Aloya said, who had only sipped her drink.

'Thank you,' Lord Neasdon said. 'I knew it would please you.'

He spoke in an intimate, possessive manner which made Craig tighten his lips. Then as a steward started to refill the glasses he said to the Baron.

'You have not told me, Baron, and it is something I would like to know, why you have brought two yachts with you to Monte Carlo.'

123

The Baron hesitated as if he was thinking up some good explanation, and as he did so there was a sudden clatter as one of the Russians fell forward onto the table, his forehead coming to rest on a saucer and the coffee in his cup slowly pouring out onto the white cloth.

The Baron turned his head angrily and said something sharply to the man next to him which Craig even with his limited knowledge of Russian knew was a rebuke for a disgusting example of drunkenness.

But as he spoke the other Russian collapsed too, and because his face was turned towards the Baron, he fell sideways and before anyone could realise what was happening he had slipped under the table.

The Baron looked absolutely furious, then as he opened his lips to speak, Craig said very quietly:

'Do not blame them, Baron, the Tokay they drank contained a drug which works instantly. They will sleep for the next three hours, then be left with nothing more than a very unpleasant headache.'

The Baron stiffened and his fingers clenched slowly into his palm.

'As your two "friends", as you term them, are unable to enjoy the rest of your visit here,' Craig went on, 'I suggest their place be taken by another guest on your yacht, Mr. Randall Sare.'

'I refuse, I absolutely refuse!' The Baron replied.

'Very well,' Craig said. 'If you will not send for him I will take the *'Mermaid'* out to sea, and there will be a most unfortunate accident on which the two Russians who are here with you as your body-guard will not be able to report coherently in any detail.'

He paused before he added:

'A wheel-chair can so easily slip overboard.'

There was a long silence. Then the Baron said surlily:

'Very well, I will send for Randall Sare, but you will get little sense out of him.'

'That is my concern,' Craig replied.

He must have rung a bell as he finished speaking, for a steward came into the room carrying a blotter on which there was a piece of writing-paper engraved with the name of the yacht, an ink-well and a pen.

'You will write,' Craig said as it was set down in front of the Baron, 'telling whoever is in command of the *'Tsarevich'* to bring Randall Sare here in my motor car which is waiting at your gangway. One man can help him, or two if necessary, and although it is only a very short distance, the car will make it unnecessary for him to make the effort to walk if he is not fit enough to do so.'

The Baron's lips were tight with fury but he wrote in a scrawling hand on the writing-paper and signed it with his name.

Then he put down the pen and Craig picked up the paper and handed it to Aloya.

'See that the Baron has written exactly what I said, and that there are no hidden instructions of which we are not aware.'

She read it very carefully. Then she said:

'I think it is all right.'

Craig took it from her and said to the Baron:

'If by some forethought you have left instructions that, if Randall Sare should be sent for or in any other way taken from the prison in which you have incarcerated him, he is to be killed, let me make it quite clear that if he does not come here alive, then your life will be forfeited for his.'

'You would not dare . . .!' the Baron exclaimed furiously.

'I would not bet on that,' Craig replied very quietly, and it seemed to Aloya watching him as if he somehow grew larger and exuded a power which menaced the Russian.

For a moment the eyes of the two men met as if in conflict, then the Baron looked away first and he said gruffly:

'Sare will come, but we will get him sooner or later, Vandervelt, and you!'

'I should imagine it is a very outside chance,' Craig replied lightly.

He called the steward back into the room, handed him the note which he had put into an envelope, and without waiting for any further instructions the steward left.

Craig rose from the table.

'I suggest, as it is rather depressing to sit here with your two unconscious countrymen, Baron, that we move into the Saloon which will be more comfortable. I am sure you would like a glass of brandy with which to finish the meal, and perhaps take away the taste of Tokay.'

He glanced at the Russian with his head still lying on the table as he spoke, then as Aloya rose Lord Neasdon said as if he could no longer contain himself:

'I demand an explanation as to why I was not told that this sort of thing was going to happen!'

'The only explanation I am prepared to give will be in a report to your superior at the Foreign Office, and I hope for your sake he listens sympathetically.'

The warning note in his voice made Lord Neasdon go pale, and when they had moved into the Saloon he threw himself down petulantly in a chair as if he could not bear to look at his host or Aloya.

He picked up a newspaper, and it was only after he had been pretending to read it for several minutes that he realised it was upside-down.

The Baron was silent, and Craig knew he was thinking desperately of how he could avenge himself for what was an unexpected coup.

Craig however, was primarily concerned with Aloya, and as if she knew what he wanted she walked down the Saloon looking at the pictures, discussing them with him, and inspecting the books of which there was a large shelf-ful in one corner.

After what seemed a long time but was actually quicker than Craig dreamed possible, his secretary opened the door to say:

'The car has arrived, Mr. Vandervelt.'

Craig walked without speaking to the door where he could see Randall Sare stepping out from the car.

There was one Russian already on the Quay waiting to help him and another following.

They each took his arm as he walked the few steps towards the gangplank, and Craig knew it was not only to be of assistance, but also to keep him prisoner in case he should try to escape from them.

When they reached the gang-plank there was room only for one person to move up it at a time, and one Russian walked ahead with Sare like a sandwich between him and his colleague.

He stepped aboard and as he did so a sailor who had been standing to attention put his arm around his neck to pull him backwards, and Craig moved forward with a swiftness that came from years of practice and pulled Sare out of the way of the man behind him.

He was fumbling for the gun that was in his pocket, but he was too late.

Before he could get hold of it he was in the vice-like grip of two sailors, and both the Russians were carried quickly out of sight while Craig drew Randall Sare into the Saloon.

He put his arm around him protectively as he did so and realised that he was very thin, almost emaciated.

He saw too there was a look on his face which meant he had not completely readjusted himself to life and was still dazed from being in the spiritual world into which his trance had taken him.

Then as they entered the Saloon and somebody shut the door behind them Aloya gave a cry of happiness:

'Papa!'

She threw her arms around her father, and he smiled at her and it was as if the clouds moved away from his eyes.

'Are you all right, my darling?'

Randall Sare's voice was low and very hoarse.

'I should be asking that of you, Papa,' Aloya said and tears were running down her cheeks.

'I am all right,' Randall Sare replied, 'but still a little bewildered.'

Craig helped him into a chair.

'Sit down,' he said, 'and I will bring you a glass of champagne, but what is more important, I know, is that you require food.'

'Yes, you must be very hungry,' Aloya said.

Even as she spoke a steward brought in a bowl of soup on a silver tray and set it down beside him.

'Light and nourishing,' Craig said with a note of laughter in

127

his voice. 'I remember you told me that a long time ago, and I have not forgotten.'

'You have a good memory, Craig,' Randall Sare said, 'and I received you message last night.'

'I thought you would.'

The two men's eyes met for a moment and they knew how closely attuned they were to each other.

Then as Aloya knelt at her father's feet, slowly as if he knew it was a mistake to hurry, he sipped small spoonfuls of the warm soup.

Craig went back to stand in front of the Baron.

'I think, Baron,' he said, 'although it seems a pity that our acquaintance should end so abruptly, I should send you back to your yacht. My car is outside waiting to carry you there, and your friends will be ready to escort you. The two other gentlemen who are still asleep will be left on the Quay and can be collected by your own men, or left to be picked up by the Police.'

He saw the expression of anger on the Baron's face and added;

'Your body-guards will leave behind them some offensive weapons which, may I point out, are not usually carried by gentlemen when they attend a luncheon party.'

Craig was aware that the Baron was now shaking with fury at the way he spoke and his hands were clenched so tightly that the nails were digging into his palms.

But he was completely powerless, and that was more humiliating to a Russian than anything else.

Craig rang a bell and as the door was opened instantly by his secretary, he said:

'Have the Baron conveyed to my car, and when he is actually inside it allow the last two Russians to join him.'

As his secretary advanced into the room Craig said to the Baron:

'We are leaving now, but should you consider following the *'Mermaid'* with either or both of your yachts, I will save you the necessity by saying that our speed is about double yours, and there is no possible way you can catch up with us, and as you are eager to do, make yourself objectionable.'

There was a provocative note in his voice as he continued:

'Go now, otherwise I might regret that I did not dispose of you when I had the chance. But you will live to fight another day, and that should be some satisfaction even though Randall Sare's secrets remain in British hands.'

Now as if he could no longer contain himself the Baron swore under his breath volubly and furiously in Russian.

Only Aloya understood, and she made a little murmur of protest.

Then at a signal from Craig the secretary moved the Russian swiftly from the Saloon and the door closed behind him.

There was the sound of engines starting up beneath and it seemed only a moment later, although there must have been enough time to get the five Russians ashore, there was the sound of the gang-plank being brought on board and the *'Mermaid'* started to move out to sea.

It was then, as if he had been too angry until now to ask questions, that Lord Neasdon enquired:

'Where are we going? Where are you taking us?'

'We are going first to Nice,' Craig replied, 'and because I have no wish to spoil your holiday in the sun, I wil put you ashore there.'

He thought Lord Neasdon looked slightly apprehensive, and he said contemptuously:

'You need not be afraid, the Russians have no further use for you, and I am absolutely certain that by the time you return their two yachts will no longer be in Monte Carlo harbour.'

'They will not . . follow us?' Aloya asked nervously.

'There is not a chance,' Craig answered. 'Those old-fashioned yachts take a long time to get up steam, and by the time they do we shall be miles away along the coast.'

'I suppose it is unnecessary to ask where we are going,' Randall Sare said.

'I am taking you to safety,' Craig answered, 'which was the first thing I was told to do. The second was to rescue Lord Neasdon, a new member of the Foreign Office, from the wiles of a Russian spy.'

Aloya gave a little laugh, and Lord Neasdon said angrily:

'That is a lie!'

129

'I am afraid it is . . true,' Aloya replied. 'I was . . spying on you, but not very . . effectively.'

'I cannot believe it!' he said. 'Do you mean to tell me you were simply trying to extract information when you said all those things to me?'

There was a stricken note in his voice which made Craig for the first time, feel rather sorry for him.

'What I am going to suggest, Neasdon,' he said, 'is that we leave Sare and his daughter together and go on deck to look back and make quite sure the Russians do not have some fantastic new weapon of which we have not yet heard by which they can either follow or sink us.'

He spoke laughingly and he knew what he said did not make Aloya in the least afraid, but Lord Neasdon looked worried as he rose from the chair in which he was sitting.

Then as if there was nothing else he could say, he left the Saloon followed by Craig.

They walked out on deck and Lord Neasdon muttered;

'I cannot believe it! It is incredible! I thought she cared for me.'

'She was forced by the Russians, to play the temptress,' Craig said, 'and when you have been in the game as long as I have you wil learn that one must never take chances.'

'How was I to know? How was I to guess that she would deliberately spy on me and tell me all those lies?'

'She was trying to save her father. She told me how desperately sorry she was at having to deceive you, but Sare's life was at stake.'

'Do you believe they would have killed him?'

'Yes, after they had tortured him.'

'I did not know such things happened in the modern world!'

'In your new position in the Foreign Office,' Craig said, 'you will find things can be very different from anything you have experienced before in the comfortable Embassies of Europe.'

'How do you know all this?' Lord Neasdon asked aggressively. 'After all, you are American.'

'Even Americans have their uses at times,' Craig replied, 'and incidentally, we never ask questions of one another, nor do

130

we ever reveal what we are doing or have done, or from whom we receive our instructions.'

He spoke sternly, like a School-Master to a young pupil and Lord Neasdon looked abashed.

Craig walked onto the bridge where the Captain was navigating the ship and said:

'Show Lord Neasdon our latest gadgets, Captain. I know he will be interested.'

'It'll be a pleasure, Sir!' the Captain replied, and there was nothing Lord Neasdon could do but pretend to show an interest he was far from feeling.

Craig left him and went back to the Saloon, and as he joined Aloya and her father, she said:

'How can you have been so . . wonderful . . so marvellous as to have . . saved us so cleverly. Papa and I do not know . . how to thank . . you.'

'You can both thank me very easily and very adequately,' Craig said.

They looked up at him and he said to Randall Sare:

'I think you know that the sooner Aloya and I are married, the safer she will be!'

CHAPTER SEVEN

Craig watched Lord Neasdon being rowed ashore in the boat which had been summoned from the harbour by a signal. Just before it arrived he said quietly:

'When you write your report for the Foreign Office, if you say that you were aware from the very beginning that the Countess Aloya Zladamir was not what she appeared to be and you were curious to verify what you suspected to be the Russians' intentions, I shall not dispute it.'

Lord Neasdon, who had been looking extremely depressed, seemed to become more alert. Then he replied:

'Do you mean that?'

'I mean it for two reasons,' Craig replied. 'First, because I can understand all too well what you felt for the Countess, and secondly, I would not wish to be instrumental in damaging what I am sure will be a brilliant career.'

'That is very generous of you,' Lord Neasdon said.

There was no time for more. The sailors were letting down the rope-ladder by which he was to descend into the boat, and he only paused to hold out his hand.

'Thank you, Vandervelt,' he said, and there was no doubt that his gratitude was sincere.

Then as the rowing-boat moved away Craig said to the Petty Officer standing beside him:

'Tell the Captain full speed ahead!'

As he spoke Craig went below.

When he joined Randall Sare and Aloya in the cabin and said that the sooner she was married the safer she would be, Randall Sare's eyes had lit up for a moment.

Then before he could speak, his head dropped on his chest and he murmured a little above a whisper:

'I – am so – tired.'

Craig did not wait to argue. He knew that Randall Sare had been buoyed up to exert himself far too soon after coming out of the trance, and now exhaustion had set in.

He merely picked him up his arms and carried him below as if he was a child, followed by Aloya.

The moment they appeared Craig's valets came hurrying from one of the cabins and he said to them:

'I want you to undress Mr. Sare and get him into bed as quickly as possible. Do not disturb him. He is asleep.'

As he spoke he was aware that Randall Sare's head was on his shoulder and he was in a deep sleep from which it would be difficult for him to wake for a long time.

One of the valets opened the door and Craig carried him into an extremely comfortable cabin, beautifully furnished and decorated, as were all the cabins in the yacht, with valuable pictures of ships.

He laid him down very gently on the bed, and as his second valet joined them he took Aloya by the arm and drew her from the cabin out into the passageway.

'Will Papa be . . all right?' she asked.

'I promise you he will be, although he may sleep for twenty-four hours before becoming conscious. But he has had something to eat, and that is all that matters.'

'And . . you saved . . him!' she said in a little voice that broke on the words.

He took her along the passage into another cabin which she realised was Craig's private Sitting Room, where he could escape and be alone if he had guests who occupied the main Saloon.

In it was a desk, a sofa, two comfortable red leather armchairs and a magnificent picture of a battle at sea between an English man-of-war and a Spanish galleon.

But Aloya had eyes only for the man who stood beside her, and she said still in the little broken voice she had used before:

'How can I . . thank you for . . saving us? How can I . . tell

133

you what it means to . . know that . . Papa is no longer in that evil man's . . hands?'

'I will show you how you can thank me,' Craig answered.

He put his arms around Aloya and drew her to the sofa, and as they sat down his lips were on hers.

He kissed her passionately, demandingly, as if he was still afraid of losing her.

To Aloya it was as if she had been taken from the depths of Hell into the celestial light of Heaven.

She could hardly believe there was no longer any reason to be afraid that her father would be tortured and killed, and she herself would be left in the hands of his murderers.

But for the moment it was difficult to think of anybody but Craig, the sensations he evoked in her and the wonder of his kisses.

Only when he raised his head and looking down into her face saw in her a new beauty springing from her happiness, did she manage to say:

'I . . love you . . I love you . . I want to kneel at your feet and . . thank you for being . . so wonderful. There are . . no words to tell you what I . . feel.'

'Your lips express that far better with kisses,' Craig answered, and even to himself his voice sounded strange, deep and unsteady.

He knew that never in the long list of his love affairs had he felt as he was feeling now.

It was not only that he desired Aloya as a woman and her beauty thrilled him, but he felt they were so closely attuned to each other that their vibrations linked them as one person, and it was difficult to think that even marriage could bring them any closer than they were already.

As if his thoughts conveyed themselves to Aloya she said:

'Did you really mean . . as you told Papa . . that we should be . . married?'

She spoke a little shyly and the colour rose in the magnolia whiteness of her cheeks.

'Of course I intend to marry you,' Craig said, 'but only, my darling if you are willing to do so.'

134

'Are you really asking me such an .. absurd question?' she asked. 'I can imagine nothing .. more perfect than to be married to you, if you .. really love me.'

'I love you as I have never loved anybody before,' Craig answered, 'and this is true, Aloya, although you may find it hard to believe, I have never in my life said "I love you" to any woman but you!'

'Is that .. true?'

'I swear it is the truth because I have never found anybody who is so completely perfect for me, and you knew just as I did that our vibrations linked us together long before you allowed yourself to love me.'

She gave a little sound of happiness and hid her face against his neck.

He kissed her hair before he said:

'How can I have been so fortunate as to find you when I least expected it?'

As he spoke Aloya gave a little laugh and asked:

'How could you .. love me when you .. thought I was .. spying for the .. Russians?'

'My instinct told me that you were not doing it willingly,' Craig replied, 'but even if you had been, I would still have loved you, and would have been unable to escape from you.'

She looked up at him, and suddenly the radiance in her face was replaced by one of fear.

'Suppose,' she said, 'the Baron .. carries out his threat and kills both .. you and Papa?'

'He will not do that.'

'How can you be so certain?'

'I will tell you later,' Craig replied. 'I want to talk about you, and tell you how much I love you, and to hear you tell me that I am the only man you have ever loved.'

'That is easy,' Aloya replied, 'because I did not know love could be .. like this until I knew you .. and found, even though I refused to acknowledge it, that you .. were in my .. dreams.'

'As you were in mine.'

Then he was kissing her again, kissing her until they were

135

no longer on the yacht, but flying towards the sun, and the golden glory of it was in their hearts, their bodies and on their lips.

A century later, or so it seemed, there was a knock on the cabin door, and Craig took his arms from around Aloya and went to open it.

His valet stood outside, and knowing the man wished to speak to him he went into the passage, closing the door behind him.

'Mr. Sare is all right?'

'He's still asleep, Sir, and we've made him comfortable. But those devils had slashed him with their knives and burnt him with cigar ends!'

Craig's lips tightened. This was what he had expected the Russians would do when they were trying to find out whether Randall Sare's trance was feigned or real.

Because he knew that both his valets were experienced in treating wounds he asked:

'You have attended to him?'

'I've done what I can for the moment, Sir,' the valet replied, 'but the best thing he can do now is sleep, and every time he wakes I'll give him something nourishing to eat, so that he dozes off again.'

Craig nodded and said:

'I am sure you two will take it in turns to sit with him.'

'Of course, Sir.'

The way the valet spoke made it sound as though he was offended that Craig should have thought even for a moment they would do anything else.

'Thank you,' he said. 'You realise of course that I have no wish, unless it is absolutely necessary, to call in a doctor. There might have to be explanations which I would prefer not to give in this part of the world.'

'Leave everything to me, Sir, and don't let the young lady worry about him.'

'I will try,' Craig replied.

As he spoke he knew it would be a great mistake for Aloya to know how her father had been treated, but once again, because they were so closely attuned, when Craig went back into the cabin she asked:

'Is Papa all right? The Russians have not . . harmed him?'

'He will be all right,' Craig said soothingly. 'My valets are both trained in nursing a sick man and can do it very much more effectively than most doctors.'

'That means they have nursed you when you have been . . injured on a mission . . like Papa.'

'I could never aspire to do the marvellous things your father has done,' Craig answered. 'I am only a humble pupil following along the path behind him.'

'I know you are much more than that from the way Papa spoke to you,' Aloya said perceptively. 'And if you had not saved him I know they would have taken us back to Russia, and we would neither of us . . ever have been . . free again.'

There was a note in her voice which told him she was perilously near to tears, and Craig held her close against him as he said:

'As your father's daughter, you know as well as I do that once a mission has been successful it is better never to refer to it again, and certainly never to be afraid of what has been prevented from happening. I want you to forget all about it and concentrate only on me.'

'That is easy,' Aloya said, 'because I love you more than the whole world, and there is . . nothing else but you . . and you . . and you!'

The way she spoke was very moving, and Craig could only kiss her until there was nothing else for either of them but the beat of their hearts, and a love which could only be expressed by their lips.

Because Aloya was very happy and her love had made her radiant, Craig was certain she would sleep peacefully that night.

He, on the other hand, would have to spend several hours writing a confidential report on what had happened which would go into the archives at the Foreign Office and be seen by only two or three Senior Ministers who were actively concerned with the problem of Russia's encroachment on Tibet.

Later as the afternoon came to a close and the sun sank, having finished a very English tea in the Saloon, Aloya said:

'I suppose you realise I have nothing to wear except for the clothes I stand up in? I am only hoping that one of your valets may be able to provide me with a tooth-brush.'

Craig smiled.

'Come and see your cabin,' he said. 'I think when I designed it I must have been thinking of you.'

She gave him an entrancing smile and he could not help adding:

'Once we are married, you will share my cabin which is larger, but it needs a feminine touch.'

She looked shy and he thought the blush that swept over her face was the loveliest thing he had ever seen, but she slipped her hand into his as he took her to the cabin which was opposite his Sitting Room.

As he opened the door she saw that the walls were Nile Blue in colour and the bed was draped with coral curtains, which the Egyptians used in many of their Temples.

'It is lovely!' Aloya exclaimed.

Without speaking Craig opened one of the panelled walls which concealed a large cupboard and she saw to her astonishment that all the gowns which the Russians had provided her with to entice Lord Neasdon were hanging there.

She gave a cry of amazement, then looked at Craig for an explanation and he said:

'You understimate my powers of organisation! I thought it was poetic justice, if, having been provided by the Russians with such an expensive and elaborate trousseau for their own ends, you should continue to use it until I can buy you, as I intend to do, the most beautiful clothes any woman ever possessed.'

'But . . how did you manage to get . . hold of them?' Aloya asked.

'Before I left the Hotel,' Craig explained, 'I instructed my two valets to go to your room and pack everything that was there.'

'But . . surely Olga – my Russian maid – tried to . . stop them?'

Craig gave a little laugh.

'I believe she spoke very volubly on the subject,' he replied, 'but my men silenced her.'

He saw an expression that was almost one of horror on Aloya's face and added quickly:

'They did not harm her. They merely gagged her and tied her up, so that she was obliged to watch them taking away your things! On my instructions they left the Baron's jewellery behind, heaping it into her lap so that there could be no question of her later accusing them of theft.'

He spoke with such a note of amusement in his voice that Aloya could not help laughing.

'I can hardly believe it!' she said. 'Olga was a very . . frightening . . overbearing woman.'

'I imagine it may be some time before she is discovered by the chambermaids, probably just about this time of the day.'

Aloya gave another little laugh and put her arms around his neck.

'How can you think of everything?' she asked. 'I shall always be frightened that you will find me inadequate as a wife, and certainly as a housewife.'

Craig's arms tightened about her.

'You are everything I have ever dreamed of, and that is the only thing that matters.'

He kissed her until a sudden movement of the ship made them sway on their feet, and he said:

'I want you, my darling, to make yourself beautiful for me, although I think it is impossible for you to look any lovelier than you do at the moment. But in half-an-hour's time I shall know I was mistaken!'

'In half-an-hour!' Aloya exclaimed. 'I need all that time in which to change, so leave me quickly.'

She was laughing, and because she looked so adorable Craig kissed her again until she pushed him away and shut the door behind him.

As he went to his own cabin he knew that never in his whole life had he been so happy, while every nerve in his body seemed to glow as if with an electric spark.

When Aloya joined him upstairs in the Saloon, night had

fallen and the stars were coming out in the sky.

The sea was calm, and the lights from the yacht were reflected in the water, while the lights along the coastline made a picture that was so beautiful that Craig thought it would always remain in his mind.

But when Aloya came into the Saloon he knew that she was lovelier to him than any view he had ever seen in his life, lovelier than the snows on the peaks of the Himalayas, the sun rising over the desert, or even the moonlight on the Taj Mahal.

Almost as if India had been in Aloya's mind when she was dressing, she was wearing a gown that was not unlike a *sari*, draped over one shoulder and gathered round the waist.

As if the designer had tried to capture the mysterious depths of her eyes, the material was of a very deep mauve, embroidered with silver and ornamented with stones like amethysts.

It was a lovely gown, but Craig had eyes only for the translucence of Aloya's skin, the silver of her hair and the light of her eyes that told him far better than any words how much she loved him.

They stood for a moment looking at each other, then she ran across the cabin as if only in his arms could she be safe and secure.

'You look very beautiful, my darling,' he said.

'That is what I wanted you to say,' she answered.

They had so much to talk about at dinner that they sat for a long time at the table after the stewards had left them. Then Craig drew her from the Saloon out onto the deck and they stood together looking up at the stars.

'How could I have been so stupid as to think for a moment that God and the Power in which we both believe would not save Papa and me?' Aloya asked in a small voice.

There was a pause. Then she went on:

'I am ashamed now that I was so frightened . . and yet there seemed to be no way out . . no chance of survival until I . . found you.'

Craig remembered how when he had listened to her talking to Lord Neasdon she had seemed like a small animal caught in a trap and trying vainly to escape from it.

Because it hurt him to remember how anxious he too had been

140

when unable to solve the problem of Aloya or to find Randall Sare, he put his arms around her protectively and looked up at the stars to say:

'We must have faith, and that is something the world needs; the faith that we are never really alone and the Power is always there if we choose to use it.'

Aloya drew in her breath.

'You understand,' she said, 'and I thought there would never be another man in the world who would think as Papa does.'

'We have so much to learn,' Craig went on, 'and because we will do it together, my darling, it will be more exciting for me than it has ever been before to explore the unknown and find the secrets of the Universe which are hidden except to a chosen few.'

'And you are one of them,' Aloya said softly.

Because he was afraid she might get cold he took her below and said:

'Tomorrow we shall be in Marseilles, and I want you now to go to sleep and not worry about anything.'

She looked up at him and he knew she was longing to ask questions, but unlike most women because she guessed he wanted to keep his plans secret she was silent.

Then she said softly:

'I must say goodnight to Papa.'

'Of course,' Craig answered.

He opened the door of the cabin in which her father lay sleeping and as soon as they appeared the second valet who was on duty went outside to leave them alone.

Although in the dim light Randall Sare looked pale and emaciated, the expression on his face was one of peace, and Craig knew that he was sleeping naturally.

Aloya stood looking at her father for a moment, then she went down on her knees beside him.

Softly, and as if she knew he could hear her in the dream-world into which he had gone, she said:

'We are safe, Papa, and I am thanking God and Craig for saving us. I am happy, far happier than I have ever been in my whole life, since now we need no longer be afraid.'

The way she spoke was very moving.

Then she hid her face in her hands and Craig knew that her prayers were too private even for him to hear.

He waited until she rose from her knees, and he thought as she did so that she had such a spiritual look of rapture and joy on her face that it must have been the way in which St. Dévoté had looked when her soul had flown up to Heaven in the shape of a dove.

As he thought of the Saint he sent up a little prayer of thankfulness for the help which Father Augustin had given him.

He knew that a very large sum of money which he had instructed his secretary to leave for Father Augustin before he joined the yacht would be of inestimable benefit, not only for the poor of Monte Carlo, but for all those who were hiding there for some reason and went in fear of their lives, as Randall Sare had done.

Then he took Aloya to her cabin and kissed her goodnight, and only when the door was shut behind him did he find that his whole body was throbbing with the emotions she had aroused in him.

He knew that unlike all other women with whom he had been intrigued and infatuated she stimulated his mind.

More important, his soul combined with hers until they reached out together towards the spiritual that was beyond the comprehension of ordinary people who had no idea that the things that interested and aroused them actually existed.

'I have found what many men seek, but which always remains out of reach,' Craig thought before he fell asleep.

. . . .

The following morning Aloya awoke knowing that she had slept deeply, anad her dreams had been so happy that she found it hard to come back to consciousness.

She was sensible enough to know that, since this was the first time for many nights that she had slept without fear, she felt different both mentally and physically from what she had felt for a long time.

Then she became aware that the engines were no longer throbbing under her, and knew they must be in harbour.

She rose, went to a porthole and pulled back the coral pink curtains that covered it. Seeing the Quay she knew that they must have reached Marseilles while she was still asleep.

Because she felt it was urgent for her to see Craig to make sure he was there, she started to dress wondering what time it was.

She was in fact astonished when she learned that it was already almost noon, and she had slept for nearly fourteen hours.

'Craig understood that was what I needed,' she thought. 'He thinks of everything! How can any man be so wonderful?'

She rang the bell and when one of Craig's valets appeared she asked first:

'How is my father this morning?

'He's had a good night, Miss,' the valet replied. 'He woke twice and I gave him some soup which I'd kept hot through the night, and he drank it and went back to sleep again.'

'He is sleeping now?'

'Like a baby, Miss. Don't worry about him. I'll fetch your coffee.'

The valet disappeared before she could ask him about Craig, and while she waited she wondered if he was as anxious to see her as she was to see him.

When the valet returned with the coffee she managed to say:

'Does Mr. Craig know I am awake?'

'The Master's gone ashore, Miss,' the valet replied, 'but he'll be back soon, and he said if you asked for him he wouldn't be very long.'

Aloya therefore dressed herself in one of the pretty gowns which the French designer had told her proudly would be the talk of Monte Carlo.

She remembered how she had hated the idea then of strange people staring at her and also being humiliated and ashamed that she was being decked out in order to attract a man so that she could extract from him information that was required by the Russians.

'If you do not learn from him what we wish to know,' the

143

Baron had said bluntly, 'we will take your father away immediately, and you will never see him again.'

Aloya gave a little cry of horror and he had added:

'It is up to you. Make this man your lover. A woman can extract anything she wishes to know from a man once they are in bed.'

'How can you expect . . me to do anything so . . horrible . . so despicable?' Aloya had faltered.

The Baron had merely looked at her in a way which made her feel as if she was a slave, naked in the Market Place, and he was assessing her price.

She had known only too well that when they tortured her father for the information they required of him, there would be nothing she could do to save him.

Her only hope therefore was to play for time and pray for some miracle that they would be able to escape from the Russians before they were taken away from Monte Carlo.

She therefore set out to attract Lord Neasdon as the Russians had told her to do, playing on his vanity and telling him how attractive she thought him, but being afraid that it was only a question of days before she had to become his mistress.

Every word she uttered, every moment she was with him had made her feel as though she wallowed in the filth of the gutter, and yet there had been no other way in which she could save her father.

It had seemed like a light from Heaven, or rather the Arch Angel Michael, when Craig had appeared and her instinct had told her she could trust him even while she was afraid to do so.

'One word to anybody outside,' the Baron had said, 'one cry for help, and your father dies!'

But her instinct had told her that Craig could save her. She had known even in the first few minutes when he had spoken to her on the balcony that he was different from any other man she had ever met.

There was something within herself which reached out towards him and made her feel that they vibrated to each other and were close in a manner that she had known before only when she was with her father.

144

But while she prayed that he could save them, her mind warned her that one unwary step, one indiscreet word, and she would have signed her father's death warrant.

At night when she tried to sleep she had thought of the Power that her father had told her was always there, and she tried to believe him.

At the same time she had been terrified that she might do something wrong because she was so inexperienced.

Then the miracle had occurred and Craig had defeated the Baron and outwitted the men who had guarded her father both by night and by day. He had been so clever that even now it was hard to believe it had happened without bloodshed and without anybody being injured.

'I love him!' Aloya had said in her heart. 'Please, God, make him love me.'

Her intelligence told her that there must have been many women in Craig's life. He was so handsome, so attractive, and Lord Neasdon had told her enviously how rich he was.

But her instinct told her that all that was of no importance and they had something so precious, so sacred and unique which they shared between them that nothing else was of any consequence.

She was waiting on deck when she saw a motor car being driven along the Quay, and then Craig stepped out of it followed by the Captain of the yacht.

As he came up the gang-plank her first instinct was to hurl herself into his arms, but with a superhuman effort she stood waiting until he joined her.

They looked at each other and somehow there was no need for words. They were as close as if their lips were touching and a kiss joined them.

Craig did not speak. He only took Aloya by the hand and drew her into the Saloon.

Then he stood with a smile on his lips looking at her, and she said almost childishly:

'I . . I was waiting for . . you.'

'I thought you would be, but it took a little time, my darling, for us to be married.'

145

She stared at him incredulously and he said:

'In accordance with the law of France we have been married by the Mayor of Marseilles, with the Captain acting as a very able proxy for you.'

'I . . I am . . married to . . you?'

Aloya's voice seemed to come from a very long way off.

'We are married!' Craig replied. 'But because I know it will please you, I have been to the Russian Church to arrange for us to be married again in the faith to which your mother belonged later in the afternoon.'

Aloya gave a cry that was also a sob, and the tears were in her eyes as she said:

'How could you . . do anything so . . wonderful? It is something I want . . more than . . anything else.'

Craig put his arms around her but he did not kiss her and merely said:

'I think both of us know that we have a faith to which all religions aspire, and the Power in which we both believe, my darling one, does not depend on any particular creed. At the same time, I want to see you as a bride, and I know you will feel that you are even more blessed than you are already if you hear the words spoken in your own Church.'

Aloya drew in her breath.

'I . . wanted that,' she whispered.

Then Craig was kissing her freely, demandingly, possessively.

It was only after luncheon that she said:

'It seems a somewhat banal question, but what would you wish me to wear?'

Craig laughed.

'I thought sooner or later you would become feminine enough to ask that! While there will be nobody present except two witnesses at the ceremony, at which the Priest will hold the crowns over our heads, I suggest we celebrate our Wedding Day in a manner we shall wish to remember, and which undoubtedly will delight our children.'

He waited for the little expression of shyness that he knew would come into her eyes, and the blush on her cheeks

146

before he laughed and said:

'A Frenchman always marries in full evening dress, and that is what I intend to wear. But I would like you, my darling, to wear the silver gown in which you look like a shaft of moonlight, and which you wore at the Grand Duke's party.'

He drew her close to him as he went on:

'It was there, unless I am mistaken, that you became aware that you could trust me, and I seemed different in your mind and in your heart from any other man you have known before.'

'I . . loved you . . and I know now that I . . loved you,' Aloya replied, 'but because it was so . . strange . . and because I have never known love before . . I felt as if you had come from the stars to help me, and for the first time there was a light at the end of the long dark passage in which I was incarcerated.'

'That is what we have found together,' Craig said quietly, 'the light that will never leave us, and which will be ours for all eternity.'

. . . .

When they knelt side by side in the small Russian Church with its hanging silver lamps and its walls covered with sacred Icons, Craig thought that the blessing of the Priest came in the form of a light.

It was the light that burned from their souls, and the light which would reveal to them both the wonders of the Universe because it was so much a part of their love.

Because the Service had been very moving and for the time being the sanctity of it swept away their passion, they drove back to the yacht in silence, and Aloya knew that in becoming Craig's wife she had reached a harbour of safety that she had never thought would be hers.

They stepped on board to find the Saloon decorated with white lilies, and when Aloya saw a huge white wedding-cake on the dining table it was impossible not to laugh and feel as if the whole atmosphere was ringing with wedding-bells.

'We are married! We are really married!' she cried.

'I will make you sure of that, my darling,' Craig said in a low voice.

147

They drank champagne with the Officers who toasted them and wished them good health, and after they had given the crew a generous ration of rum the cake was cut and sent to their quarters.

When Craig had ordered a bouquet for Aloya, he also had a wreath of small lilies made to encircle her head which was covered with a lace veil.

After the Officers had gone they sat for a while in the Saloon, then without speaking, since words were unncessary, they moved down below just as 'The Mermaid' slipped her moorings and moved out to sea.

'Where are we going?' Aloya asked.

'I do not want to stay in harbour feeling that there are people all around us,' Craig answered. 'There is a little bay not far along the coast where we will anchor for the night, and there we will be very quiet with only the stars above us and the soft lap of the sea below.'

'It sounds . . very romantic,' she whispered.

'That is what it will be, my darling,' Craig promised.

He led her not to her cabin but to his, and here again she saw there were white lilies beside the bed, and huge jars of them on the floor where they could not spill over.

As she looked up at Craig in gratitude she thought that only he could have organised their wedding so beautifully, and although it was so quiet and secret it was being celebrated in a manner which neither she nor he would ever forget.

Very gently he took the wreath and veil from her head, and as she looked up at him with eyes that seemed to be filled with stars he said:

'This is your Wedding Day, my darling, and because I love you, and because I know you are very young and innocent, I would not do anything that would spoil our happiness or make you feel afraid.'

Aloya gave a little laugh of sheer joy.

'How could I be afraid of you?' she asked. 'I understand what you are saying to me, and I am very ignorant of love because I have always lived in such strange places with Papa and Mama. But I have dreamed of it, and I know that you are the man who has filled my dreams, and . . we have been together in other . . lives.'

'I love you!' Craig said. 'I love you so much that it is hard for me to understand how one small person could completely change me overnight, and arouse in me emotional sensations I had no idea I was capable of feeling.'

'If I can give you something . . new and . . different from anybody else, that would be the most . . wonderful thing that has ever . . happened to me.'

She put her head against his shoulder as she added:

'You are so handsome, besides being so kind and so clever and so vital, that I am afraid . . after a little while . . you may find me . . boring.'

'That would be impossible!' Craig said. 'How could I be bored with myself, which is what you are, my adorable wife, not only because we have been joined by the Sacrament of Marriage, but because our bodies are one, as well as our minds, our hearts, and our souls.'

Aloya put up her arms to him.

'We are married and we are one,' she said, 'but you are the bigger and more important part of us. I shall love you and worship you for the rest of my life.'

'You must not say such things to me, my precious!' Craig protested. 'At the same time that is what I feel about you, and so even in that we think the same!'

They heard the anchor being dropped and then there was no longer the sound of footsteps overhead but only the quiet of the night and, as Craig had said, the lap of the sea against the ship.

As Craig was kissing her he undid her gown and lifted her onto the bed. She realised he had pulled back the curtains from the porthole and now there were not only the stars, but the light from a young moon climbing up the sky.

She felt it was like the life that they were starting together, with a light of such beauty and glory to guide them that it was impossible to express it except by love.

Then Craig came to her and she felt his body against hers, his heart beating on hers, and his hands touching her.

149

The moonlight not only covered them with its silver light, but vibrated within them, and it was the Power of Love that had been theirs in the past and would be theirs in the future and for all eternity.

. . . .

It was three o'clock in the afternoon and the sun was very hot when Craig, after swimming in the sea, climbed back onto the yacht to join Aloya who was resting under an awning.

He dressed himself in a towelling robe that reached the ground, and put a towel round his neck before he sat down beside her in a deck-chair.

'Do you feel cooler now, darling?' she asked.

'Much cooler.'

'While you were swimming they told me that Papa has woken up, had a good meal and gone back to sleep. But later he would like to see us both.'

'We will talk to him when he wakes,' Craig said, 'but I hope it will not upset him when we leave Marseilles tonight by train.'

Aloya gave an exclamation.

'We are . . leaving tonight?'

'I want to take you to England,' he replied, 'first because the Foreign Office are desperately anxious to see your father and find out what he has to tell them, and secondly because as soon as this business is finished, I am taking you both to America.'

Aloya looked at him a little anxiously and he said:

'I want you to meet my family and, because I think your father should disappear for a while, I cannot think of a better place for him to be than on my Ranch in Texas!'

Aloya's eyes widened but she did not speak and he went on:

'As soon as he is strong enough I am going to make him write down a great many things he will publish later, which will be of inestimable value to the world, and it will keep him busy until, in his own words, he can "get back to work".'

Aloya gave a little sigh of happiness.

'You seem to have it all planned.'

'I have a feeling that your father will agree with me that this is for the best.'

'Suppose I disagree?' she asked provocatively.

'Then I shall kiss you, my beautiful darling, until you change your mind.'

His eyes rested on her lips as he spoke and she felt as if he was already kissing her and seeing the fire in his eyes she felt a little tremor like a shaft of sunlight run through her.

She thought that they could never look at each other without feeling a response that was, she knew, the vibrations of love seeping through them.

Never had she imagined that love could be so wonderful or exciting, and at the same time so divine that she knew that everything they did was sanctified and part of God.

'I love you!' she said, and knew it was what Craig wanted to hear.

Then as if it suddenly struck her she exclaimed:

'You said that Papa must get away secretly . . but why? You do not think the Russians . . might be . . pursuing him?'

There was a touch of fear in her voice that Craig had heard before and he covered her hand with his as he said:

'I thought you might ask that question sooner or later, and because I cannot bear that you should be afraid, my darling, there is something you should know.'

'What is it?'

Craig picked up one of the newspapers which his secretary, Mr. Cavendish, had put on a low stool beside Aloya's chair when he had been swimming.

She knew he had been back to Marseilles to fetch them, but she had not shown any particular interest, feeling she had no wish for the outside world to encroach on them while all her thoughts were concentrated on her husband and their happiness.

Now Craig opened the newspaper and folding it handed it to Aloya.

For a moment, because she felt it was vitally important to both of them and she was a little apprehensive, the black printed words seemed to swim in front of her eyes. Then she read:

151

'On Wednesday evening fire broke out on the Russian yacht 'The Tsarina' which was anchored beside another Russian yacht, 'The Tsarevitch', in Monte Carlo harbour.

It was nearly thirty minutes before fire-engines could reach the ship, and by that time the fire had gained a firm hold, and a large part of 'The Tsarina' was badly damaged.

In the panic that ensued the owner, Baron Strogoloff, was unfortunately not rescued from the flames, and when they were under control his body was found in the Saloon where he had obviously fallen from his invalid chair.

It is with deep regret that we announce the death of the Baron, a distinguished Russian nobleman. It was his first visit to Monte Carlo and he was known to be a regular patron of the Theatre and a lover of music.

Several members of his crew received major burns and two of the Russian guests were taken to Hospital where they are reported as being out of danger and as comfortable as possible.'

Aloya read the report and gave a little gasp.

'The Baron is dead!'

'He will not be deeply mourned,' Craig said quietly.

The way he spoke made Aloya look at him sharply.

'You were . . responsible for . . this?'

'I did not want you to be worried,' he answered, 'and go on feeling that the Baron was threatening your father or me. Whatever reports he intended to make on Randall Sare have, I imagine, been burned with him.

He continued with a note of sarcasm in his voice:

'If I am not mistaken, the Baron would wish to have had all the glory of having captured and imprisoned such a notable character, so very little will be known of what has occurred by the Secret Police on whose orders he was acting.'

'Is that . . true?' Aloya asked.

'I am sure of it,' Craig answered. 'I know the way they work, and I was certain when the Baron was forced to hand over your father there would be consternation among his personnel and the bow of the 'Tsarina' would be left unguarded. I therefore had one of my men go on board, and they were unaware of it.'

'How did you manage that?'

Craig smiled.

'The Russians were inveterate talkers. They talk and talk about everything. I gambled on the fact that when the Baron sent for your father, they would be too busy talking about it to think of anything else.'

'So while that was happening your man climbed on board!'

'He is a brilliant electrician and also a very efficient underwater swimmer,' Craig said. 'I gave him ninety seconds to tamper with the electric wiring aboard the Russian yacht and render it exceedingly dangerous, but he told me proudly that he had taken only sixty. Then he swam back to the *'Mermaid'*, and nobody had the slightest idea he had ever been there.'

Aloya put out her hands.

'You are so . . clever that you . . frighten me.'

'Now you need not be frightened by anyone else,' Craig said, 'and we can do anything we want to do.'

Aloya's eyes twinkled.

'I think, as it happens, it will be what . . *you* want. How can I possibly oppose or argue with anybody as . . brilliant as . . you?'

Craig lifted her hand to his lips.

'I have the feeling that we shall argue and confront each other and stimulate each other's mind. It will be very exciting, but it will always end in the same way.'

'With my giving in?' Aloya smiled.

'No, in being aware we both want the same thing,' he replied. 'This morning nothing matters except that we love each other. It is going to take me a lifetime, my precious darling, to tell you how much and how greatly I love you!'

He rose from his deck-chair as he spoke and putting out his hands pulled her to her feet.

'I am going below to dress,' he said, 'and I want you to come with me, firstly because I cannot bear you out of my sight, and secondly because I want to kiss you.'

The way he spoke the last words told her they meant a great deal more than what he actually said.

She looked at him with adoring eyes. Then she let him lead her along the deck and down below.

They went into their cabin and shut the door, and he took her in his arms.

'The last cloud has been swept away,' he said, 'and if I ever see you looking frightened again, I shall be very angry!'

'How could I be really frightened of anything now that you and Papa are safe?' Aloya asked. 'Oh, darling . . darling Craig, will you promise me whatever Papa wants to do in the future, you will stay with me? I do not think after all we have been through that I could think of you in . . danger and not . . want to . . die.'

Craig did not answer. He only took her in his arms and kissed her.

Then as he felt her lips soft beneath his and, as he felt the fire that burnt within him evoke a flame within her, he lifted her in his arms and laid her down on the bed.

Then he was kissing her demandingly, passionately, fiercely, and the flames leapt higher and higher.

As they were carried up together into the sky, they knew that the divine fire of love burnt away not only fear but evil.

Now ahead of them was a happiness in which there was no fear, no danger, but only the ecstacy, the perfection and the glory of love.

THE END

A SHAFT OF SUNLIGHT
by Barbara Cartland

The moving story of Giona, a beautiful young girl who has been starved and cruelly beaten by her uncle, and who is discovered by the Duke of Alverston. To Giona, the handsome Duke becomes a messenger sent by the gods to rescue her . . .

0 552 11930 X   95p

LIES FOR LOVE
by Barbara Cartland

The entrancing story of Carmela, who takes her friend's place at the home of the autocratic Earl of Galeston and becomes involved in intrigue and danger is told by Barbara Cartland, currently the world's topselling authoress.

0 552 12127 4   £1.00

A PORTRAIT OF LOVE
by Barbara Cartland

From Barbara Cartland, comes an exciting new story about the beautiful but impoverished Fedora Colwyn, who plans to help her sick father pay off the family debts but instead finds herself implicated in a murder.

0 552 11876 1   95p

A TOUCH OF LOVE
by Barbara Cartland

From Barbara Cartland, one of the most romantic and internationally famous writers, comes a moving tale of a girl who softened the heart of a tyrant with a touch of love.

0 552 10744 1   95p

TOUCH A STAR
by Barbara Cartland

From Barbara Cartland comes the engrossing story of Lina, spirited young daughter of the Earl of Wallingham, who, escaping from an arranged marriage, applies for the post of a lady's maid – and finds herself involved in a plot to dupe a French roué – The Duc de Saverne . . .

0 552 11969 5   95p

WISH FOR LOVE
by Barbara Cartland

The adventures of the lovely and intrepid Mariota and her brother Jeremy, whose brief careers as highwaymen bring them drama and love is told in this exciting new story from Barbara Cartland.

0 552 12208 4   £1.00

THE POOR GOVERNESS
by Barbara Cartland

The beautiful and impulsive Lara takes the place of her friend as governess to the niece of the Marquis of Keyston. How she brings happiness to her lonely charge – and to the cynical and autocratic Marquis – is told in this gripping story by Barbara Cartland.

0 552 12168 1   £1.00

THE PROUD PRINCESS
by Barbara Cartland

From Barbara Cartland, one of the most romantic and internationally famous writers, comes the touching story of a young and beautiful Princess whose pride would not allow her to love . . .

0 552 10229 6   95p

BARBARA CARTLAND ROMANCES
AVAILABLE FROM CORGI BOOKS

While every effort is made to keep prices low, it is sometimes necessary to increase prices at short notice. Corgi Books reserve the right to show new retail prices on covers which may differ from those previously advertised in the text or elsewhere.

The prices shown below were correct at the time of going to press.

☐	12127 4	LIES FOR LOVE	£1.00
☐	12168 1	THE POOR GOVERNESS	£1.00
☐	11787 0	DOLLARS FOR THE DUKE	95p
☐	11840 0	WINGED MAGIC	95p
☐	10169 9	NEVER LAUGH AT LOVE	95p
☐	10168 0	A DREAM FROM THE NIGHT	95p
☐	10228 8	THE SECRET OF THE GLEN	95p
☐	11876 1	A PORTRAIT OF LOVE	95p
☐	10229 6	THE PROUD PRINCESS	95p
☐	10255 5	HUNGRY FOR LOVE	95p
☐	10745 X	LOVE AND THE LOATHSOME LEOPARD	95p
☐	10786 7	NO ESCAPE FROM LOVE	95p
☐	10305 5	THE DISGRACEFUL DUKE	95p
☐	10602 X	PUNISHMENT OF A VIXEN	95p
☐	11930 X	A SHAFT OF SUNLIGHT	95p
☐	10549 X	A DUEL WITH DESTINY	95p
☐	11136 8	WHO CAN DENY LOVE	95p
☐	10690 9	THE LOVE PIRATE	95p
☐	10744 1	A TOUCH OF LOVE	95p
☐	11045 0	LOVE CLIMBS IN	95p
☐	11097 3	A NIGHTINGALE SANG	95p
☐	10803 0	THE SAINT AND THE SINNER	95p
☐	10903 7	LORD RAVENSCAR'S REVENGE	95p
☐	10902 9	THE CHIEFTAIN WITHOUT A HEART	95p
☐	10946 0	THE RACE FOR LOVE	95p
☐	10994 0	THE DUKE AND THE PREACHER'S DAUGHTER	95p
☐	11027 2	LOVE IN THE CLOUDS	95p
☐	11969 5	TOUCH A STAR	95p
☐	12009 X	FOR ALL ETERNITY	£1.00
☐	10804 9	THE PROBLEM OF LOVE	95p
☐	12068 5	SECRET HARBOUR	£1.00
☐	12085 5	THE VIBRATIONS OF LOVE	£1.00

ORDER FORM

All these books are available at your book shop or newsagent, or can be ordered direct from the publisher. Just tick the titles you want and fill in the form below.

CORGI BOOKS, Cash Sales Department, P.O. Box 11, Falmouth, Cornwall.

Please send cheque or postal order, no currency.

Please allow cost of book(s) plus the following for postage and packing:

U.K. Customers—Allow 45p for the first book, 20p for the second book and 14p for each additional book ordered, to a maximum charge of £1.63.

B.F.P.O. and Eire—Allow 45p for the first book, 20p for the second book plus 14p per copy for the next seven books, thereafter 8p per book.

Overseas Customers—Allow 75p for the first book and 21p per copy for each additional book.

NAME (Block Letters) ....

ADDRESS ....

....